Paws

SANDRA KLEIN

PAWS

2006

Paws

THANK YOU!

I would like take this opportunity to thank all that have helped me in some way while I wrote this book.

Chris, you are the best friend one can ever hope to find in their life. Your kindness and love has no boundaries. Don't ever change!

I would like to thank Sherry for all the talks, the good advice and for the final touches on the book. I could not have done it without you. You know you will always have my love.

And last but most importantly my biggest gratitude goes to Steve. You told me I could do it. You believed in me before I did and I love you dearly for it. Thank you for being my friend.

Sandra Klein
July 2006

Dedicated To My Father

INTRODUCTION

L et me begin by introducing myself. My name is Sandra and I just love cats. At the moment I have 7 cats but there was a time when I had as many as 12.

What most people don't know is that cats live a life beside that of being a pet(s). They have schools, stores and businesses just like we do. I just happened to find out about all this from my oldest cat, Clubby. I caught him talking on the phone one day, when I came home at an odd hour. He had no choice but to tell me all about his daytime (and nighttime) activities. I can tell you, it's quite amazing.

Since I now know about this "other" life, the other cats also tell me everything that goes on. At a certain point I started to keep this diary on all my cats and their activities.

Come and join me in the wonderful world of my cats. Meet Aristotle, Bear, Goofy, Luke, Mozes, Jimmy and Maya. These are the seven cats who have taken up residency in my house at this moment. But you will also read the stories about Clubby, Cindy and Max. And of course how could I ever forget Mickey and adorable Katinka?

I hope you enjoy it.
Sandra

1.

Paws

Today I came home and asked Bear how his day had been. He told me it was great and that he had purchased the most amazing thing; a paw. I said "a what?" He said "a paw" and he showed it to me. You know how we humans have pda's otherwise known as a Palm? Well cats have a paw. It's basically the same device we use but smaller, and of course especially designed for cats.

He told me it would be great to help him keep stock of his inventory, and his appointments with the suppliers. Perhaps this needs a little more explaining.

You see, Bear has a nightclub. A very successful nightclub, I may add. Bear is not only owner and manager of the club but he also performs there. A one cat show, so to speak. Sometimes he takes one of the dogs and puts him into the act. That is something really spectacular. My dogs are big dopes and wouldn't hurt a fly, but the other cats don't know that. He brings them on stage in a cage, so it all looks very dangerous. And then he lets them out of the cage on the stage and then he jumps over them, puts his head in their mouth, etc.

Imagine a circus with a tiger act, you get the idea. You should hear the audience when he does that, they go wild. However the dogs don't really like it, so he can't do it that often. Besides, the dogs have to be bribed big time. I once had the privilege of having a peek into the nightclub. There are very comfortable beds and seats where the cats can sit or lay down when they want to. There is also a small dance floor. That's not used very much though. However Goofy is a very good dancer. He sometimes gives a dance show. You wouldn't guess it if you see him, because he's a bit plump and very lazy, but when he starts to move, ooh man!

Bear

The bar serves milk, hot or cold, kit bits and things to nibble, but you can also have a full meal there. The menu varies from regular to deluxe at which point they serve fresh fish or gourmet food. Bear has one bartender and two female waitresses working for him. The bartender is a big burly male, who also serves as bouncer.

One other thing surprised me in the nightclub. There were little pieces of wood on the tables. They were little planks, with a piece of elastic attached. So I asked Bear what those were for. He looked at me with one of those "you stupid human" looks and asked me if I had ever heard a cat clap.

I did not want to make a smart remark by telling him I had never seen a cat nightclub either, but I resisted the temptation. I just simply said I never had, and he explained to me that when cats applaud you hear nothing. Well, maybe a slight whooshing of paws. So they designed these planks which they put on their paws (hence the elastic) and then clap them together.

But I digress. As Bear showed me all the features on his new paw it wasn't long before all the other cats were standing around us. Of course they all wanted to see it. And, sure enough the inevitable happened; at a certain point they were all pulling at the paw, wanting to play with it. So Bear stepped in, grabbed his paw and walked away. "It's mine, go buy your own!" he shouted as he walked away, leaving all the others behind looking disappointed.

Within a few seconds, up came the cries. "We want a paw, we want a paw" they mewed. Well I put an end to that dream immediately. I told them that since they don't have their own business they don't need a paw. Of course they disagree. Let me tell you - never get into a discussion with a cat. You can't win. Their logic is beyond a humans' comprehension. My husband has warned me many times. Every now and then he walks in on me having a discussion with one of them and he just shakes his head. Sometimes he mumbles something like "I told you NOT to do that?" But I can't help myself.

So while I stand there discussing the paw issue with them, Bear walks in with a bag. Turns out he went to the store and bought everyone a paw. Sometimes he is so sweet. You can imagine everyone's happiness as they scurried off to their own corners with their new found treasure. He even gave Maya one. What is she going to do with a paw? She's only four months old. I said to Bear that I thought he was very sweet but that disaster was just around the corner. "You know that, don't you?" I asked him. He just shrugged and walked away. At the door he turned around and said "that will be your problem then." Nice huh? He's smart, that Bear. He makes sure to be out of reach before saying something like that, because he knows I get angry. But I can never stay angry for long. They are just so cute when they're naughty.

As I had predicted, within the hour there was trouble in paradise. Maya came running up to me, crying her eyes out. After I had calmed her down, she finally was able to tell what happened. Jimmy had managed to break his paw (within an hour!) and he had gone over to Maya and took hers away. So of course she was terribly upset. Poor thing, it's not easy living as the only female with all those males. Jimmy is just a year old and he has been teasing Maya since the day she arrived. I think he likes her, but he just shows it in a very bad way.

But for now, I had a crying kitten on my lap. So I asked if she really liked that paw so much. She thought for a while and concluded that she really did not know what to do with it. "So it's not so bad you don't have one anymore" I suggested carefully. That just got her started all over. "But now I am the only one without a present" she cried. So I asked if she would like to go to the store and pick out a toy she wants. That was the best suggestion I could ever have made. She immediately stopped crying and nodded happily. Now I am not going to let a little kitten go to the store all by herself, so I called Goofy.

He is always willing to do such errands for me. I gave him some money and told him to take Maya to the store. I told him she could pick out anything she wanted. It is always such a fun thing to see, when Goofy takes her by the paw and takes her out. It's fun to see them walking away in the morning on their way to school like that.

I was hoping that my suggestion had the problem solved, which it did, but it also created a new problem. Maya came home dragging a plush rabbit behind her. I looked at Goofy and asked him how things went. He just looked at me and walked away. Of course I went after him and asked what had happened. "I don't want to talk about it" was his answer and he ran into the garden. So I asked Maya if everything was alright. She told me everything was fine and that she was not aware of any problem.

I must say I am very curious to know why Goofy is so angry...

2.
Plush rabbits

Yesterday before we went to bed I told Maya to make sure her rabbit was inside the house. Everything left outside during the night is confiscated by the dogs. The dogs also have toys that squeak and are fluffy so they will not know the difference between their toys and Maya's rabbit.

This morning when I woke up, I opened the door and guess what? Maya's plush rabbit ripped to pieces! Oh my goodness! Quickly I picked up all the pieces and put them in the garbage. If Maya sees that ripped rabbit she'll be hysterical. After I finished hiding the evidence of the rabbit murder, I went over to Goofy and told him that he had to go get the same rabbit at the store for Maya. He almost went into a fit. I still had no idea why he came home so upset yesterday, so I told him that he was the one who brought Maya home and as such she was his responsibility. Well that didn't work, so I offered him money. That helped. Muttering and still very angry, he left for the store.

There is perhaps something I should tell you about Goofy. He runs a kitten school. He has the perfect character to run a kitten school. But he has very little business sense and as a result he hardly makes any money with the school. I asked him once why he did not charge a bit more. He told me it was no use since he had to give everything to his brother Aristotle anyway. But that is an entirely different story.

One day Goofy came home from school with a 5 week old kitten. He told me he had found her at the gate of the school and that she had no parents or owners. So he took her home with him. "You have so many cats already, one more won't hurt." I thanked him for being so thoughtful but the sarcasm was lost on him. So that is how Maya came to live with us and every now and then I try to use the "you brought her here" remark on him when something happens or she does something bad.

While Goofy was on his way, Maya came to me. "I can't find bugs anywhere." "Who?" I asked, trying to look clueless. Apparently she named the rabbit "Bugs". I think she watches the cartoon channel too much. I told her that it must be somewhere and that she should keep on looking. After ten minutes she was back with the announcement that she still couldn't find him. I told her she had not searched really carefully since she was finished in just ten minutes. Of course, I had to help looking, which I pretended to do. But at that moment Goofy came in, with a bag which he handed to me.

I opened it up and there was a plush rabbit inside alright, but it wasn't the same size. "Goofy, this is not the same one" I cried. He told me it looked exactly the same and that it was only a bit bigger. "She won't know the difference" he assured me. "If you say so" I replied and I walked away to hide the rabbit somewhere so Maya could find him. And sure enough she did. Happy, she came running to me and showed me the rabbit. "I found him mamma" she cried happily "But he seems bigger than yesterday." I sighed, that darn Goofy! I told her that perhaps Bugs was still growing just like she was. You have to think quick sometimes with these cats. That had her thinking for a couple of seconds. "That must be it" she finally said and walked away, pulling the rabbit behind her. What a relief she's so gullible.

With that crisis out of the way I went in search of Goofy. I was going to find out why he was so upset about that toy. I found him in the kitchen, sleeping. First I tried to softly tickle him and get him talking in his sleep. It sometimes works. However this time he was just napping, so not really asleep. He sat up and looked at me real disgusted. "You are a sneak, mamma" he said to me. Since I was in no position to disagree I told him that he forced me to it. "You're the one not telling what's going on." He sighed deeply, "If I tell you, will you drop it?" I swore not another word would be said about the subject. So he told me Maya had embarrassed him terribly in the store by picking a people toy. Now I did not understand how she could buy a people toy in a cat store. But let me tell you something; never ever tell your cats you don't understand something. To them it's all very logical and they do not really have the patience to explain anything. You might as well just act as if you understand, because you are never going to get it anyway.

So I answered hesitantly "I see..." but Goofy wasn't buying it "no, you don't. You're just saying so." "Well then, why don't you humor me, my dear" I replied as sweetly as I could. Words like "honey" and "dear" always soften Goofy up. After a big sigh he explained that the cat store also sells people stuff in case a cat wants to buy something for his or her owner. That got my eyebrows raised. They never got me any gifts and when I ask them why not, they always tell me the store doesn't have anything for humans. I said nothing about that but just asked why that was such a bad thing. "Because cats don't buy people toys for themselves! That's why. I just hope no one saw me. I won't hear the end of it"

So I asked him why Maya picked a people toy in the first place. He explained to me that she wanted the same bunny as I have in my room (I collect stuffed animals and the loony tunes characters are one of my favorites). And it is true that every time Maya comes into our bedroom, she immediately starts playing with my stuffed animals. I nodded in comprehension. "Why don't you just tell everybody that Maya bought that rabbit for me?" Now there was a thought that had not entered his mind before. He put up his thinking face and finally said "Okay. Now can we just forget about it?" "Sure, Goofy, and thanks for buying the rabbit for Maya." He gave me a "yeah, yeah" look and walked away.

I am going to make sure that plush rabbit is inside during the nights from now on. I don't think I can get Goofy to go out and buy another people toy.

3.
Rabbit trouble

few days have gone by since the rabbit tragedy and I thought the dust had settled. I was wrong. This afternoon I heard an enormous ruckus in the living room. I ran in, only to find one of the dogs holding Maya's rabbit by the ear, the other dog holding the rabbit by the legs and Maya in between pulling at the rabbit. In the meantime she was crying and yelling and every now and then she would try hitting the dogs on the snout. Of course she was hoping they would let go. What she didn't know is that this just encourages them more.

One word from me was enough for the dogs to let the rabbit go. I picked it up and checked it out. Luckily it was not damaged... yet. Meanwhile Maya was jumping at my feet for her rabbit. As soon as I gave it to her, she ran off, yelling and swearing at the dogs. The dogs were just standing there, wondering why the fun had stopped. I told them that they shouldn't play with someone else's toys. They told me they didn't know it was Maya's. Of course that resulted in a question from me if they have never seen Maya playing with it in the last few days. "Uh, yes we have" was their answer. "And you didn't think that perhaps it was hers?" Now those are not questions you should ask a cat or a dog. Like I said before, their logic is not our logic.

Trying to get into their logic, I asked "where was the rabbit when you found it?" "On the couch" was the answer. "And where was Maya at that time?" You know what they told me? They said she was sleeping next to it with her paws around it. Amazed I asked if that shouldn't have been a clue for them. Thinking back it should have, but at that point they just wanted to play, so they didn't think. "Well that's just the problem, isn't it" I said angrily "you guys don't ever think, do you?"

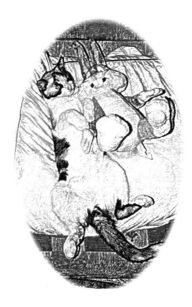

That was a big mistake. They started telling me about all the times that they did think. I looked at them in amazement. "You're kidding me right?" But they weren't and continued summing up all the times they had thought. I was at the point of walking away, when Goofy came in. The dogs got him involved in the discussion. Goofy, kind as he is, also confirmed that there were times when the dogs did think. To stop this ridiculous conversation I finally said "Just keep your paws off Maya's toy in the future, will you?"

They stopped in the middle of their enumeration and asked if I did not want to hear the rest. I just shook my head and walked away. Sometimes I get so tired of these animals. At times like these I wish I never walked in on Clubby that day, I would not have known anything about all this and would have been spared a lot of aggravation. But you can't change the past now, can you?

Anyway, an hour later I walk into the kitchen to find it filled with rabbit stuffing. I looked around me in amazement, looking for Maya. I found her behind the kitchen island with her rabbit. It goes without saying that I asked her what was wrong. She told me that she didn't know. She had taken her rabbit with her to take a nap and when she woke up she saw that there was something sticking out of the rabbit. "There was all this white stuff coming out of him, so I started pulling at it." "And now?" I asked while she was looking very sad at an empty rabbit. She held the rabbit up and stated "I think he's broken." I saw her eyes already filling up with tears so I quickly offered to fix the rabbit. "Can you?" she asked hopefully. I told her I could always give it a try.

I collected all the filling and the limp rabbit and started putting everything back. While I was busy at the kitchen table, Goofy walked in, sat in front of me and looked at me. He gave me one of his "told you so" looks, so I turned away. He followed. Finally I looked up and said "what?" He told me that this was why he was against her buying a people toy. I reminded him of the fact that he told me it was because he was embarrassed by it. "No, I also told you that they break easily." I carefully tried to remind him that he had never said such a thing, only that he was so very humiliated when Maya picked that toy. "Yes, but I also told you they break easily."

"No, you didn't."

"Yes, I did."

"You said nothing about breaking."

"Well, that is what I meant."

"Excuse me? Now I have to read between the lines?"

"How do you do that?"

"What?"

"Read between the lines? There is nothing there."

"It's an expression."

"What?"

"Read between the lines is an expression."

"But there is nothing there?"

"I know there's nothing there, it's just a saying."

"Why do you read it when there's nothing there?"

"Goofy, leave me alone."

"So, you just want me to shut up just because you can't admit I warned you?'

"About what?"

"That rabbit"

Heavy sigh...

I told you that you can't win an argument with a cat, ever. I ignored him and continued stuffing Maya's rabbit and sewed it up. She was so very happy when I gave it back to her. Goofy just sat there looking at me. I knew he wanted to say something more to me, but I really did not feel like getting into another discussion. "Momma" he finally said "next time don't let Maya buy a people toy." I looked at him, to see if he was kidding. "You bought her that toy." "Perhaps, but you told me to, so it's your fault." I told him to let the matter go, but he insisted on asking me one more question.

Against my better judgment I let him. "Remember those cat toys we have in the living room?" Of course I know those toys, I bought them. I wanted to know why he asked. "Are they broken?" "No, they're not." "Well, then I rest my case" he concluded, got up and walked away.

4.
Fire

This morning while I was standing in the kitchen, preparing breakfast, I saw a completely black cat walking in. Now I don't have any black cats. I have two black and white, two grey and white, two reds and one tri-color kitten. But this cat came walking in as if he did that every day, so I took a closer look. Turns out it was Bear. He jumped up on the table and started to eat his breakfast. After he was done I asked him what had happened.

He told me he had been busy cleaning up the night-club for the better part of the night. I was amazed. That must have been some clean-up. I told him I never realized cats were such "pigs". But that was not the case. Turns out there had been a fire. Luke had been begging Bear to let him do an act in the nightclub. "That was not such a good idea, looking back" Bear said. "Really?" I asked. He gave me a rather dirty look. What was the act you're wondering? Luke had a juggling act. First rather innocent with hoops and sticks and balls, but then he lit the sticks and put on an amazing fire act. However he dropped one of the sticks and the stage caught fire. No one was hurt, since Bear had just upgraded the entire nightclub to meet the latest safety requirements. The sprinklers put out the fire rather quickly, but it still did enough damage.

Bear was obviously very angry at Luke. So I asked him if Luke had asked permission to do his fire act. He said that Luke had told him that everything would be alright and not to worry about a thing. "Well, why did you not stop him, when you saw him lighting those sticks?" Bear sighed "I was too far away to do anything. By the time I got to the stage it was already on fire." I felt so sorry for Bear. "How come you're all black, dear?" I just had to ask. Well he had been cleaning up all the smoke damage and clearing out the burned stage.

I took out a napkin, moistened it and cleaned Bear up a little. He did not really appreciate it, especially with the water and all. I just told him to suck it up and that he would thank me later. "I doubt it!" was his friendly answer. "Is there anything we can do to help you build a new stage?" I asked trying to calm him down a bit. It helped. He thought about the offer and said he would get a drawing of what he wanted.

That same evening I heard a lot of noise and racket in the back yard. So I went out and I saw several cats jumping over the wall and Luke and Mozes standing there. Their backs all arched, the tails all big and fluffy. "What's going on here?" I demanded to know. Apparently some cats had come to make fun of Luke because his act failed. I sighed and told them that they should know better than too fight about something like that. "Next time just tell them that if they know how to do it better, they should try." I was a bit surprised to see Mozes there at the side of Luke. Luke is a bit of a street fighter. Mozes on the other hand is soft and sweet and would not hurt a fly. I asked him if he too was fighting. "Oh no" he said "I was just trying to talk to them" "Oh talking, shmalking" Luke said "You know you can't talk to cats that are high on catnip!"

"All the more reason to let it go, Luke" I tried, but he was still very upset about the insults. Suddenly he ran after them. I tried calling him back, but he wouldn't listen. I guess he didn't hear me. "I think Yoga lessons would be good for Luke" I heard Mozes say as I was staring in the direction Luke had run off to. "Yoga lessons?" I said, as I turned to Mozes. "Yes, Yoga lessons. It relieves stress and anger and makes you all mellow." "But you don't have any stress, Mo?" I was amazed. Like I said, Mozes (or Mo as I sometimes call him) is the sweetest thing you could ever meet. "No, because I do Yoga" which was, of course, an answer I could have seen coming from miles away. "When did you start this Yoga?" I asked while we both walked back to the house. "Hmmm, I think a month ago"

"A month ago?"

"Yes"

"But you have no stress whatsoever in your life, Mo"

"Because I do Yoga"

"Yes, but two months ago, you also had no stress."

"That was before I started Yoga."

"That is correct. So why start Yoga classes?"

"To get rid of all the stress I had."

"But you had no stress, dear"

"That's because I take Yoga lessons."

"No, no you misunderstood me. I mean you never ever had any stress to begin with."

"Thanks to those wonderful Yoga classes."

"Mo, listen to me. Did you have stress before you started the Yoga classes?"

"Of course, otherwise I would not need it."

"And how did you know you had stress?"

"Well, because I needed Yoga classes."

"And how did you know you needed Yoga classes?"

"Because I was stressed."

"They also brain wash you during those classes?"

"Huh"

"Never mind dear, just go do your Yoga exercises."

It went on for a bit longer than what I just told you but suddenly I felt this huge headache coming up, so I stopped. I think I might need some Yoga classes too. As I was sitting there recuperating from this very intense conversation, I saw Luke coming back to the house. He was limping. So I ran up to him, picked him up and asked him what happened. He was grumpy and obviously very angry "put me down, let me go" he demanded. So I put him down and he limped back to the house all by himself. I followed him and let him in the bedroom. Our bedroom is normally off limits to all cats, but this time I was willing to make an exception. I sat next to him and tried to hear what had happened. I also tried to take a look at his paw that he could obviously not use. But he just growled and demanded that I leave him alone. I guess his ego got a big dent tonight.

We'll see how things are tomorrow.

5.
Luke

Well this morning Luke was still limping around on three legs, so I told him I was going to take him to the doctor. "I can go to my own doctor" he said. "I meant a people doctor, one who specializes in animals. We call them a veterinarian." "I know what a veterinarian is" Luke said angrily "and I'm not going!" "Yes, you are" and I grabbed him. He hissed and growled at me, but I ignored him. I put him on the kitchen counter and told him to wait, until I got the cage.

"I don't need a cage!" he yelled after me. "Are you going to come quietly with me then?" I asked. He looked away and refused to answer. "Well?" I said "are ya?" "Not in this lifetime!" was the answer I finally got. "Then I am going to get the cage. You sit and wait here for me."

Of course when I got back, he was not there. But on three legs he could not have gone far. I walked into the living room where I heard a soft voice say "Go away, you're going to let her know where I am. Go, you stupid dog!" I looked and saw the dogs in a corner, walked over and found Luke in the corner next to the cabinet. "Now you see what you have done!" he hollered at the dogs, when I picked him up. "But, Luke it is for your own good" the dogs cried in stereo.

I took Luke with me and sat on the couch, sat him upright and looked him in the eyes. "Now listen here, Red" I said firmly "you know very well that it is best that you go to the doctor. What if your leg is broken? Let the doctor take a look at it. Okay?" He agreed under protest. "Oh and try to behave when you are there" I said. It was a good thing I already had him in his cage at that moment, because he would have most certainly run away. "I always behave" he said coldly and turned his back to me.

So, off we went to the doctor's office. It's not a long drive, but once in the car Luke thought to be funny and started howling like a mad cat. I almost swerved the car into a light post. I looked at him (the cage was on the passengers chair) and said "I am not amused, Luke." He grinned and said "revenge is a sweet thing". He did keep quiet the rest of the way.

At the doctors' they took some X-rays and it turned out the leg was not broken. Luke was an angel during the whole thing. He let the doctor examine him and did not make a sound, even though it was clear that he was hurting him. We got some pain killers and were told that it just needed time. Back in the car, Luke had to let me know how useless this visit had been. He just kept nagging and nagging "I told you I didn't have to go. I told you". I kindly explained to him that I had to be sure. If we found out later that his leg had been broken, he could have been crippled for life. To get through to these animals you sometimes have to trick them. So I got him out of the cage hugged him and sobbed "I could not let that happen to you, Luke. Just imagine if you have to walk on three legs for the rest of your life!" I even managed to get out a tear. This got him totally upset. "I'm sorry Mommy, I did not mean to get you sad like that. I'm okay, my leg is not broken and with the pain killers I'll probably feel better." He licked the tear from my cheek and put his good paw around my neck. "Now let's go home" he said as he turned and got back into his cage. I was amazed at how well my trick had worked. "Maybe Bear can get me a wheelchair, just like the one you had, not so long ago" he said with a big smile on his face. I did not really see the fun in that, but I found out later what he was up to.

A little more than four months ago, I fell down a stair and really badly sprained my ankle and knee. It was not broken, but it might as well have been. I spent a little more than a month in a wheelchair, and after that I spent 6 weeks on crutches and as we speak I am still limping a bit. When we got home I first gave Luke his pain killer. This helped him enormously. It must have hurt really badly, if he was in such a bad mood. Well I should know, I had the same thing.

Later that afternoon he came in on crutches, which Bear obviously got him and he mimicked my way of walking with those things. "Look at me" he cried "I'm Mommy!" The other cats were all laughing so hard, tears were rolling out of their eyes. "I see the pain killers are working, dear?" I asked. He just went on with his joke, entertaining the others. "Oh, Mommy you are so funny" Maya cried while she was rolling around on her back laughing. "Me funny? Luke is acting like an idiot." All I got was more laughter. At least now I know why Luke was smiling when we were in the car. He was planning this joke all along.

I walked out of the room, sighing, wishing I had never walked in on Clubby that day. Maybe I should enlighten everybody on what happened "that day". I will, but not today. A few hours later Luke came up to me. He had gotten rid of the crutches and was looking really sorry for himself. "What is it, dear?" I asked. "Can I have some more of that pain killer, Mommy? It is starting to hurt again." I got up and took him with me to the kitchen. I gave him his medication mixed with some food and asked if perhaps he wanted his paw dressed. "Will it help?" he asked looking very doubtful. I explained him about the advantages of a dressing and he agreed "but only if you take it off, in case it sucks." I smiled and nodded.

With his dressed paw he looked even sorrier for himself than he already did. I convinced him that in a few days he would be feeling better. "A few days?" he cried frightfully "yes, Luke, a few days, maybe even longer. Remember me? I am still limping a little and I fell over four months ago." He sighed and let me put him on our bed. With the medication he was a bit sleepy and he almost immediately dozed off.

When I got out of the bedroom, Mozes was waiting for me. "Is Luke going to be alright?" he asked concerned. "He is going to be fine. He just needs to rest his leg and he will be good as new in no time." "He should take Yoga lessons" Mozes stated. "I don't think Yoga is what he needs right now, Mo." "Of course it is. Just look at me, are my paws broken?"

"No, but neither are his"

"But they are almost broken."

"No, they're not!"

"With Yoga it will be better sooner."

"Well, why don't you ask him that after his nap, Okay?"

"Ask what?"

"About the Yoga"

"Luke doesn't know anything about Yoga"

I sighed. At moments like these it is very hard to stay calm. Not only is Mozes very calm and sweet, he also has an attention span of approximately 3 seconds. I bent down, patted him on his head and said "Isn't it time for Yoga class, darling?" He looked at his paw-watch and ran off.

As an added note I can say that Luke started walking on all four legs after four weeks and he is all better now.

6.
How Clubby came to live with us

I have mentioned Clubby a few times. First let me tell you how he came to live with us. This is not "that day" but the day we got the greatest cat in the world.

Way back then, we were still studying and we went to school everyday with the train. One rainy day in September, my husband hurried to get his train. Underneath one of those tunnels leading up to the train platform he rested for a minute, while shaking off the rain. He had put his suitcase on the ground and was folding up his umbrella when out from the bushes walked this cat.

A regular cat, black and white, about 5 to 6 months old. The cat huddled against my husbands' suitcase to find some shelter against the cold wind and rain. It was obviously a stray, but at that point my husband could do nothing for him. He had a train to catch, which was already at the platform. So he picked up his suitcase, turned to the cat and said that if he was there that afternoon at 5 he would take him home and give him a good home.

My husband never thought that the cat would actually be there that afternoon. But he was. So, as promised, my husband picked him up and took him home. By the time I got home the cat had already installed himself comfortably on the couch. He was acting as if he had lived with us his entire life. It turned out the cat had taken an instant liking to the both of us and he had taken a special liking to me. He sat on my lap when I was watching television. While I was studying he would come and lie in my arms on the table, preferably on my books so I could not read a thing. He ate like a horse and very soon became a rather big cat. Not fat, just big.

It was obvious that he was an extremely intelligent cat. Whenever we would tell him to stop doing something he always did so immediately. He would come when we called him, which is very unusual for a cat. Everything new in the house had to be inspected by Monsieur himself. He would sit next to my husband whenever he was fixing the sink, the bike or whatever was broken at that moment. After "that day" he would also comment on everything and constantly ask questions. It would drive my husband mad.

He was kind of rough when it came to playing. We would have a toy mouse on a rope and drag it in front of him. He loved that! Whenever we played with him it was always all the way. He would completely let go of all the brakes. Sometimes he would smash his head into the wall or door, simply because he could not stop in time. Sometimes he would see it coming and turn his head away at the last moment and smash his body into the wall or door. It sounded like someone was hitting on the door with a baseball club. That is how he got his name; Clubby. Till this day I am still amazed that he did not break something in those younger days.

When we had Clubby for six months we decided that it was rather sad for him to be home alone all day. After all, we left in the morning for classes and did not come home till late in the afternoon. So we got Cindy. Cindy was the sweetest kitten you'd ever seen. With her black/white/red fur she was a beauty. Clubby was wild about her from the beginning and she about him. However we were not thrilled about their first meeting. Clubby instantly seized the kitten and he would lie on top of her, pinning her down with his paws on her ears. So the first three days we kept them apart. Or at least we tried. At night we locked Cindy in a separate room, afraid Clubby would make her fall down the stairs. We did not sleep for three nights. Clubby just kept on jumping on our bed, howling in front of the door. He tried to hold paws with her by reaching under the door. After three sleepless nights we gave up. It was obvious that she also wanted to be with him.

Looking back he was very careful with her; however it did not seem like it to us those first few days. The playing would always be the same: Clubby on top of Cindy biting her in her neck and trying to put his paws on her ears. As Cindy grew bigger, we started to see bits of her sticking out from beneath Clubby. First her fluffy tail, later a paw, until she was finally big enough to throw him off if she did not like his rough play. It was love at first sight and from the moment they met, they always acted as husband and wife. I once asked Clubby if they indeed got married, but in the cat community the concept of wedlock is not known. However he was faithful to her and she to him.

Cindy was always very worried if we could not find Clubby. You see he had the habit of going into the closet whenever I had to get something. Or he would follow me into a room and stay while I left and shut the door. Cindy would always be hysterical if something like that happened. She always showed me where he was. At first by howling and meowing in front of the door, later by just simply calling me to let her husband out.

Three years ago we moved from Holland to Aruba. At that time Clubby and Cindy were 13 and 12 years old. Besides being rather old, Clubby was also very sick at that point and the doctor had told us he would only have a few months more to live.

We really did not know what to do.

Finally Clubby asked how he would have to travel. I explained how he would have to be put in a cage "together with Cindy?" he asked. "No, only one cat per cage allowed" I answered. "Okay, and then what?" he demanded to know. I continued the explanation how he would have to get in his cage at around 7.30 in the morning. That was the time we would have to leave for the airport which was about an hour's drive. At the airport the cats would have to be checked in. Because we were traveling with animals we would have to check in three hours before departure. After the check in they would be put in a special section of the airplane. "It will be a nine hour flight and when we arrive, you have to go through customs which will probably take another hour" I finished.

Clubby looked at me shocked. He made a quick calculation and concluded "that means you will lock me in a cage for almost 14 hours?" I nodded, that was about right. "You know

I am not well, and you know how stressed Cindy always gets. I am not putting my wife through such an ordeal" he answered firmly. He was right of course. For a healthy cat it would be a stressful and rather trying voyage. Clubby was not well and I really did not feel good about taking him, but I was even more upset about leaving him behind.

"I can give you guys a sedative" I tried feebly. Clubby was disgusted by the thought. "I think it is best if Cindy and I find another home" he finally said.

He could not travel so far in his state and Cindy could never be separated from him. I was devastated but I knew he was right. It was the only thing we could do. So we found him a good home: a farm. We went there with him to check it out. He said he loved it; "nice and spacious" was his verdict. Clubby also immediately loved the lady who would take care of our duo. She is a woman with a heart of gold. She has no idea how grateful we are to her for taking care of our babies. Sometimes words are just not enough even though they are the only things you can express yourself with.

Two days before we left on our big journey, we left Clubby and Cindy at their new home. It was the hardest thing I ever had to do. I think I cried for three days straight. The four cats we did take with us, tried to comfort me and it did help, a little. They told me he would stay in touch with me through them. And indeed every now and then I get a message from Clubby. I don't know how they do it, but cats somehow seem to have their own communication system.

Now after three years Clubby is still alive and doing very well. So much for the doctor's prediction. However Cindy passed away about a year ago. It is believed she had a brain hemorrhage. Clubby's new mommy told me he was rather upset about it all. She also said that in the last hours of her life Cindy only reacted whenever Clubby meowed. For the rest she would just lie there before she slipped into a coma and softly passed away. She was truly faithful till the end.

Clubby is still going strong in his new house and hopefully I get the opportunity to visit him once more before he passes on. I miss him dearly every day. He is just so very special...

7.
Bribed

For the last few days, Goofy has been an absolute pain in the butt. He is constantly demanding attention. He wants to sleep on my lap, and here in the tropics that is rather hot. He asks the most stupid questions, solely to get my attention. He is also of the opinion that all of a sudden he is allowed to sleep in our bedroom. His reasoning: "because we always have." I asked if he was becoming senile or something. Rather upset about my statement he started crying. Now I was upset! Goofy has never cried in his life.

I quickly picked him up and tried to console him. I wasn't doing a very good job, because he only started crying harder and harder. At that moment Aristotle walked in. I looked at him and put on my "what is the matter with him" face. "He is having trouble with some parents" Aristotle said. So I held Goofy out in front of me "is this true?" "Yessssss" Goofy sobbed. After about thirty minutes I finally had him calmed down enough for him to tell me what was going on. Now I will give you the short version, but it took me about two hours before I understood what had happened exactly.

To give you an idea, the conversation went something like this.

"What is going on Goofy?"

"It is all Edwards fault."

"Who is Edward?"

"He is a friend of Bobby."

"And who is Bobby"

"He took Edward home."

"Who, Bobby?"

"For cat food"

"Bobby took Edward home for cat food?"

"But he didn't know that"

"Bobby didn't know that?"

"Of course Bobby knew."

"So then Edward didn't know?"

"How could he?"

"Beats me, I have no idea who Edward is, or Bobby for that matter."

"Haven't you been listening?"

Now that you have an idea of what I went through, I will give you the summary of what happened. Edward is one of the kittens at Goofy's school. Bobby is a male friend of Edward's mother, Vivian. I get the impression that Bobby is Edwards' father, but I'm not sure. Vivian, however, is one hot feline. And she has many male admirers, Bobby being one of them. So Bobby is at Edwards' home on a regular basis and definitely no stranger to their household. Now a few days ago, Vivian wasn't there to pick up Edward from school. Instead, there was Bobby. Now Goofy doesn't let the kittens leave with just anybody. He either gets them on the school bus or he waits with the kittens till one of their parents or owners arrive. Since Goofy knew that Bobby was a regular at Edward's house he saw no harm in letting Bobby take Edward home.

However that turned out to be a big mistake. Seems that Bobby is a villain cat. He befriends innocent females and then catnaps their kittens in order to get some money out of it. Of course Goofy did not know that, Vivian did not know that and Edward did not know that. Vivian could not do anything else but to pay that darn Bobby the ransom he demanded. However she is blaming Goofy for the fact that Bobby got the chance to take Edward from school. So she wants him to pay her back the ransom she had to pay Bobby. With interest!

Of course I told Goofy that her demand was ridiculous and if she wants her money let her sue. Turns out she already did that and the judge agreed with her. I think the judge fell for her pretty face. So now Goofy has to pay and he has no money. I asked him if he did not have any money from the school money all the kittens pay. He told me he gave everything to Aristotle.

Cats don't ever volunteer information so I asked why he gave everything to Aristotle. The answer was "because I have to." At this point I remembered the contract he has with his brother. You see, Aristotle is a bit of a schemer. He is always looking for ways to make money (easy money, to be exact), but looses it as easily in stupid investments. Aristotle has the knack of offering others services that he can't really provide. For example he will try to sell a rock to a lizard to live under even though the rock is already there and the lizard is already living under it. But he is one smooth talker and somehow almost everybody falls for it. He has also, from the very beginning, been talking Goofy into giving him his money. In the early days he told Goofy that he had to give him his allowance. Aristotle would in return make sure Goofy got food every night. I once told Goofy that it was not Aristotle who bought the food in this house and that he would get fed even if he did not pay Aristotle (or Ari as we call him most of the time). But Goofy just wouldn't take the chance and has kept on paying his brother throughout the years.

To stop this abuse, I just stopped giving him his allowance and only give him some money if he needed anything. That way he could tell Ari that he did not have any money and therefore could not give him any. Ari did not appreciate my action, but I couldn't care less. I told him it was wrong to take advantage of his brother(s). He did the same thing with Bear in the beginning but luckily enough Bear wised up. So much so that in the end Ari had to sell his nightclub to Bear in order to pay his dues to Bear. The nightclub has been a big success ever since Bear owned it.

I know somehow Ari got Goofy to sign a contract containing a policy that 90% of Goofy's future earnings must go to Ari. So that is why Goofy charges almost nothing for his school. Whenever he needs to renovate the school building he asks the parents to contribute by giving wood, cement, paint etc. He will then organize a day of renovating and all the parents will come and help repair whatever is broken. They always close it with a big barbeque which Bear organizes. That is his donation. These get-togethers are always a big success. Ari is not too happy about them. I'm just glad Goofy finally found a way to outsmart his brother.

But let me get back to the bribing issue. After Goofy had told me everything we just sat next to each other thinking of what had to been done. After all, Goofy was ordered by the judge to pay back the ransom money to Vivian, with interest. Out of the blue Goofy suddenly said "can't you pay it, Mommy?" I looked at him in shock. "What... you think I'm rich or something?" I replied. His conclusion was that we definitely had more money than he did, in which he was probably right. "How much do you have to pay?" He sat there thinking and counting on his paws while I heard him mumbling "plus interest comes too..." It took him a really long time before he said "four cans of cat food!" I couldn't help myself but I started laughing. While trying to stop the laughing I asked if he was serious. The answer was "yes." Goofy was looking at me, kind of lost.

Still giggling, I got up and walked to the kitchen. I grabbed two cans with cat food from the cabinet, held them up to Goofy and asked which size would do. He said the little one would be just fine. "And what if I give you the bigger one?" "That would be even better. That way she can't complain at all." So I put four of the bigger cans in a plastic bag and handed them over to Goofy. He immediately ran off to Vivian's house, dragging the bag behind him. Ten minutes later he was back, happy as a kitten. Vivian had forgiven him and told him that she would be sending Edward back to school the next day.

He was giggling like a kitten in love for the first time and had a big blush on his cheeks. I think he is smitten with Vivian.

8.
Storm

Two days ago we started having heavy thunder and lightning at around 10 o'clock at night. The cats were quite startled by the loud bangs and the enormous racket. So within minutes they were all around me. I was sitting on the couch in the living room and they all gathered on the table in front of me.

I looked up from my book and saw seven cat faces looking at me intensely. "Yes?" I asked. "Maya is afraid of the thunder", Luke cried while looking at yet another lightning bolt in the sky. "If Maya is the only one who is afraid, then why are all of you here?" I wanted to know. "We are protecting her" Goofy said as he trembled from the next thunderclap. "I see" I said as I looked at each and every one of them. "What is happening?" Maya wanted to know. I explained that there was a thunderstorm on the way. That unleashed a tumult of questions about what a thunderstorm was and what was going to happen.

I looked at the three oldest, Ari, Bear and Goofy and said "you guys have seen and heard thunderstorms before. Why are you panicking like this?" They looked at each other, rather sheepishly when Bear suddenly said "it's all Jimmy's fault. He said that the sky was falling down." I took a deep breath and looked at Jimmy who was sitting under the table terrified and trembling at every lightning bolt that came. So I asked Jimmy why he thought the sky was falling down. He could hardly say a word but I finally understood that some of the cats at his school had been telling tall tales of falling skies. So I explained to him that the sky could not fall. When I was finished all the other cats started yelling at him, that he had scared them all. I stopped them immediately. They were just as guilty of stirring up panic as Jimmy was. I especially admonished the three eldest cats as they had seen many thunderstorms in their life already.

"Well, I tried telling him…" Ari defended himself. "Did you now?" I asked sternly. Instead of answering me he looked down at his paws mumbling something like "I tried…" Jimmy looked up at me really scared and asked me if the sky wasn't falling down, what would happen? I explained to him that the lightning and thunder were caused by a thunderstorm and that pretty soon it would also start raining. I also explained that after a few hours everything would be back to normal, depending on how big the storm was. "I like water" Mozes suddenly said. This may seem very strange but it is a very true statement. Mozes does not like being out in the rain but as soon as it stops, he is out there standing chest deep in water if he gets the chance.

The other cats looked at Mozes in disgust. A cat liking water! How weird, but it did the trick. They forgot all about falling skies and all walked away and went to sleep. Not long thereafter it started raining. Quite heavily I may add.

I was standing in the kitchen when all of a sudden I heard a soft voice crying "Mommy, Mommy help meeee... As I walked into the kitchen I saw Jimmy sitting at the back door in front of the cat door. The voice was coming from outside. I asked Jimmy who was out there. He said "nobody" and quickly moved away from the door. At that moment Mozes came in through the kitty door. The poor thing was completely wet. I quickly picked him up and dried him off with a kitchen towel. "What was that all about?" I asked. "He wouldn't let me in!" Mozes sobbed, wriggled out of my arms and ran into the living room. I walked over to Jimmy and asked why he was so mean to Mozes and he giggled at his big joke. I explained that Mozes liked walking through the water but only after it had stopped raining. He doesn't like it when his head and back get totally wet. "Besides that" I continued "he could get really sick sitting out in the rain like that". Jimmy looked at me in total shock. "I did not know that. I'm sorry Mozes! It was a joke!" he cried as he ran into the living room to see how Mozes was doing.

I followed because I too was curious to see how Mo was doing. He was just fine and had installed himself on the couch in one of his yoga positions. He opened one eye and looked at me as I leaned over to see if he was still wet somewhere. "Good thing I am taking those yoga lessons, otherwise I would be completely stressed right now" He said to me. I looked down at Mozes and just shook my head. I don't think Mozes could ever be in any kind of stress. Upset? Definitely. Stressed? Never!

After four hours of heavy rain it finally stopped and the water level around our house was quickly lowering. The cats had been sleeping all through the rain, thunder and lightning and now came out to take a look. Bear looked in awe as he saw the entire front yard flooded. Never before had we seen so much rain come down in such a short time. "Wow, that is a lot of water" he said as he looked up to me "what now?" I told him that we would just have to wait till the water went down again. At this point Mozes came running onto the front porch completely excited "has it stopped raining?" he demanded to know. "Yes, it has dear." "Oh, goody" was his answer and he walked off the porch and started to enter the water slowly. Every time his paws touched the water he would shake the water from it while saying "boy, that's wet." I looked in amazement. Okay, I must admit I have seen him do that before, but it still amazes me every time. "Why go in if it is so wet, Mo?" I asked. "Because it's fun" he cried excitedly. And he continued walking, shaking his paws with every step. I watched him turn the corner. "I hope for him, it doesn't start raining again" I said as I looked at all the other cats who were sitting on the porch, looking at the water.

Of course Jimmy had to see what all the fun was about and he too went in the water. He was back in two seconds. "That pink cat is crazy" he announced while he was licking his paws dry. I had no idea cats could see colors. Mozes is indeed a bit pink. He is a sort of light red, a very strange color indeed. I dare not ask Jimmy how he knew that Mozes was a little pink. Some things are better left unknown.

Furthermore it had been a tiring night. We were on the lookout all night because of all the rain that fell. Normally we don't get that much rain in such a short time. So I was a bit tired and really did not feel like hearing some cat explanation on how they could see colors. Cats can't give you a straight answer when you ask them something, anyway.

I stood there for a while with the other cats when all of a sudden one asked me "what's that sound?" "What sound?" "That honking sound." That honking sound was a toad. "Why is he honking like that?" Maya asked. "Because he's afraid of the water" Goofy responded. "Oh, that is ridiculous, toads love water" Bear chipped in. "No, they don't. Frogs love water, toads just like it a bit wet, but not this much" was Aristotle's view on the situation.

"What is the difference between a toad and a frog?" Maya now wanted to know. "Frogs have a smooth, moist skin and have long back legs for jumping. Toads have dry, warty skin and shorter hind legs which they use for walking instead of jumping like frogs" Aristotle answered. I said nothing and just listened to the conversation of my cats. Never knew Ari had so much knowledge of frogs and toads. He continued explaining that some toads prefer living on land and if they do, their skin is colored brown. They will only come to the water to procreate. "So, then why is he honking?" Maya still wanted to know. "How should I know?" Ari snipped at her "I only know what the difference is between frogs and toads". "Mommy, why is he honking like that?" Maya asked as she turned to me. I thought for a second. "Well, perhaps he is calling for other toads to meet him" I tried hesitantly. "You mean we are going to have more of those noisy animals here?" Maya said in horror. I shrugged my shoulders not really knowing how to answer that. "You don't know why he is honking, do you Mommy?" Goofy chimed in accusingly. "I never said, I knew why he was honking" I defended myself "I just offered a possible explanation for the honking." "Well, I think that if you don't know the answer you should not say a thing" was Bear's statement. "Ari also doesn't know why he's honking" I said, trying to get the attention away from me. "Yes, but at least he admitted it" Luke had to have his say. They were ganging up on me so I had to come up with a different tactic. "Well, if one of you knows why he is honking, share it with the rest of us." That made Bear get up and walk over to the toad. He could not get completely to the toad without getting his feet wet, so I heard him shout "Why do you honk?" The only answer coming from the toad was "honk, honk, honk." Bear repeated his question a couple of times before walking back. When he reached the porch he said "stupid toad" and walked into the living room. "Now we still don't know why he honks" Maya cried. "Maybe we can find it on the internet?" Goofy proposed. "You think so?" Maya wanted to know. I turned around and while I walked away I heard Goofy say "Sure we can..."

I walked to the back door to see how the situation was over there. To my amazement I saw Mozes standing at the other side of the temporary river we had in the yard. That river was rather wide and at some parts more than knee deep. I had no idea how he got there without swimming, but he seemed completely dry except for his tummy and paws of course. He was checking things out at the other side when it started to rain again. I saw his little head pop up and he immediately turned around and wanted to get back to the house. However, apparently he had forgotten how he crossed the river in the first place. He just stood there, meowing. When they get really scared, cats forget that they can talk and they turn back to their natural way of communicating. So I called to him that he could do it and at one point I actually thought that he was going to swim. But he changed his mind and ran for the gazebo in the back of the yard. There he was high and dry and in no danger of washing away.

I felt a bit sorry for the poor thing so I called my husband and asked if he could collect Mozes. He did but when he crossed the "river" with Mozes in his arms, Mozes decided it was scary. He started to wriggle and twist. Luckily for him my husband held on tight and he did not drop him in the water. Once inside he crawled on the couch again. I asked him if everything was alright. He nodded a bit dazed after which he turned to me and said "did you see that? Daddy almost dropped me in the water!"

"No, he didn't, he held on tight so you would not fall, with all your twisting and wriggling."

"He did?"

"Yes, he did. He would never drop you in the water."

"Really?"

"Really."

"So, Daddy actually saved me."

"Yes, he did."

"That's nice."

"It is, isn't it?'

"Very…" after which he immediately fell asleep.

I looked at Mo sleeping there and thought that it might be a good idea if we did the same. After all it was six in the morning and we had not slept at all the entire night. We woke at around eleven and when I walked into the living room I saw all the cats sleeping. I walked over to Bear and asked if he wanted something to eat. He looked at me sleepily, yawned extensively and announced that he was too tired to eat. I asked what made him so tired. He told me being up all night had worn him out. "You slept through everything!" I cried stupefied.

"Did everybody have a rough night?" I asked sarcastically. Bear nodded with his eyes closed and went back to sleep.

They'll just use any excuse to sleep, won't they?

9.
Business Schemes

As you know Mozes has been going to yoga classes. Every evening, usually a little after 6, I see him running out of the house in a big hurry. When I call to him to ask where he's going he usually waves to me, signaling he has no time to talk. I did find out where he goes to yoga class which starts at six. So he's always late.

But lately I have noticed that Maya is also taking on "yoga" positions and then she falls asleep. I once asked if that was the intention. The answer I get is "you are supposed to relax and if you relax you fall asleep." It makes sense but I still believe that yoga is about something else. But I found out who gives the yoga classes; it's Aristotle. I must say at least this time he gives something in return even though it's not a whole lot. He uses Bear's nightclub for his classes. He tells all the cats to just lie down and take a relaxing position and then "relax". He sometimes has a picture of one of the yoga positions. He just leaves them there when they fall asleep and takes off. Easy money. But at least this time he does something. He did some research into yoga and is providing a service, however doubtful his reasons may be.

It got me thinking about the first time Ari got into business. He was the first owner of the nightclub. It was a great success. He had Bear perform his one cat show every night and paid him rather generously. The club became a big overnight success. There would be rows of cats outside waiting to get in. Well Ari decided that it wasn't enough so he slowly started increasing his prices for the food and drinks. After that he started to increase the entrance fee and slowly but surely the cats found their entertainment elsewhere. Most don't have a whole lot of money, so they couldn't afford the club anymore. Only a few snobs kept showing up. Of course Ari, trying to cut his losses, lowered his prices again and a few more cats showed up after that, but he had basically blown it with the outgoing cat crowd. So he stopped paying Bear. He told him to live off the tips. Poor Bear. He really liked his one cat show and hated that he had to stop. He also needed his income and couldn't do it for free. Cats are not known as big tippers.

But then Ari got himself into a whole lot of trouble. Never did find out what exactly happened but it was a business deal gone sour. So he sold the night club to Bear, who overhauled the place and it has been a great success ever since. Seemed that Bear was a very wise cat and had saved a lot of his money with which he could buy the club from Ari.

Bear was lucky with the club deal. He bargained with Ari until he only had to pay exactly that amount of money with which Ari could get out of the sour business deal. The day the deal was done Bear came home with a big smile on his face. Bear had also offered Ari a job at the club, to help him recuperate from his destitute state. But as soon as he made enough money to his liking, Ari went on his own again. Apparently he was too embarrassed to hold his paw up for money to his younger brother.

After that things went downhill. We received phone threats from so-called business partners. My Aristotle was apparently blinded by money and only looking for ways to get a lot, fast. We had to bail him out of trouble on several occasions. This was the time he talked Goofy into this deal to give 90% of all his future earnings to his brother. He also made some other questionable deals with other animals. He sold one of the trees in our garden to a bird to build his nest in. He sold "protection" against big bully cats to the smaller cats in school. When I heard about that I really had a good laugh. If you see Ari you will agree with me; he is not a fighting cat. He is a bit of a wuzz. I once asked him how he was planning on ever keeping his word on such a deal. He told me he didn't have to do anything but tell the other cats that he would call Bear to beat them up. That did the trick, he told me. Okay, well that is something I believe. Bear is not called Bear for nothing. He was twice the size of his brothers the day he was born and still is.

Things got really out of hand when he got Clubby involved in his schemes. Unfortunately for Ari, Clubby is not stupid. He is, actually, the smartest cat I've known. At first Clubby gave Ari the opportunity to set things straight, but he was so far down he couldn't. Clubby then reported him to the cat police, told him it was very unethical what he was doing. However Ari was lucky. Before they got time to do anything we moved to Aruba.

I had hoped that the threat from the police would have scared him enough to stop his obscure businesses. It did… a little. He still conducts questionable business transactions, but at least now it seems that his clients get something for their money. At least that is how it is with the yoga classes. I have been trying to stop Mozes from going to the yoga classes and try to find something useful to do. But he shows no interest whatsoever. I wonder where he gets the money to pay for the classes. Knowing that Ari gives them they can't be cheap. And now he has also tricked Maya into going to the classes.

While I was sitting out in the Gazebo writing this chapter on my laptop, Ari came and sat next to me. He was reading every word I typed. He started moving more and more uncomfortably with every word that appeared on the screen. All of a sudden he had enough and sat right in front of me, blocking the entire view of the screen. I looked at him but said nothing. "You know it is not nice talking about me like that" he finally said "and it's even worse that you try to make money of my misfortunes."

"Look who's talking. You do nothing but make money off others."

"No, I don't!"

"Yes, you do!"

"But I'm a cat!"

"Oh, and that supposedly gives you the right to trick others in business deals that are only beneficial to you?"

"The others get something in return."

"Oh, really, then what did that lizard get when you rented him that rock?"

"Well, he got a home."

"He already had a home!" I was getting desperate here.

"Okay, let me rephrase; he got to keep his home."

"And if he did not pay, you would have evicted him?"

"No, I would have eaten him."

I was stunned. Would one of my cats stoop so low? Where did I go wrong? Ari, Bear and Goofy were born in my home after I rescued their mother from certain death. I raised them from the beginning. Goofy and Bear are outstanding cats in society. But Ari??? I was totally upset by his statement. When I looked at Ari again I saw a big smile on his face. "That's not funny, Aristotle" I said sternly. He first giggled, after which he started laughing out loud. He rolled over on the table, laughing holding his paws in front of his face. Something was very funny to him, but I could not see the joke and truthfully I was getting more upset by the minute. He had gone mad!

Ari finally settled down and after he wiped the tears from his eyes he said still giggling "Boy, that was fun. You should have seen the look on your face Mommy."

"Excuse me?"

"Oh, mommy, how could you ever think I would really do something like that?"

"Well, Ari, you have been known to stoop pretty low."

"Yes, I know. But I would never go as low as murder." I must say that was a relief. "Besides that, I don't do business like that anymore. I offered that lizard protection from the dogs. Every time the dogs go after him I distract them."

"So you did not rent him that rock?"

"No, who ever gave you that idea?"

Truthfully nobody had told me, I just assumed, when I heard about "a" business deal with a lizard, that it would be something sneaky like that. So I could do nothing else but apologize. However, I still had to know about the yoga classes. So he explained to me that he did give such classes but that Mozes and Maya were his only students "and they consistently fall asleep after just 5 minutes. So I just leave them sleeping."

"You charge them for that?" "I charge them for an hour of classes. That means that if they fall asleep I only charge the minutes they were awake." "I must say Ari, I am proud of you. Looks like you have bettered your life."

"Yes, I have. That episode with the police gave me a good scare."

"Well, then you won't mind cancelling that ridiculous contract you have with Goofy?"

He gave a little giggle and explained that in the cat world no contract can ever be cancelled "just like a human marriage" he said "it's till death."

I nodded in comprehension and patted him on his head. I was not bringing up the concept of divorce. He would not understand. My Ari, I did something right when I raised him after all.

10.
Idols

Sometimes when we come home after a days work, we like to put on some music while we roam around the house. Yesterday I put on the DVD of George Michael so we had music as well as some visual distraction when we needed it.

I had been out of the living room for a while when I came back to see Maya on the salon table. She was sitting on her back legs with her front paws in the air, eyes closed swaying from one side to the other with the music of Careless Whisper. I just stood there looking at her, amazed at the fact that a cat can sit upright for so long. All of a sudden she dropped to all fours again because she noticed I was watching. "Mommy, I did not know you had music from Cat" she said to me.

"Who?"

"Cat! The greatest singer in the world?"

I thought for a while and concluded that she was most probably not talking about a human artist, so I said "enlighten me dear. Mommy can't keep up with all those new singers and bands anymore." She sighed at my total stupidity but did explain that Cat was the lead singer of the group Cat and the kitty band. I closed my eyes and tried to visualize that, but decided it was impossible. Cat is a handsome male cat who sings songs and is currently touring the world. He has a bunch of female cats that play in his band who he calls the kitties. Apparently Cat is big on the charts right now.

I also found out that Cat's real name is Bennie. But when he got famous he started calling himself Cat. A cat calling himself Cat I don't really get it, but Maya says it's "Genius!" I'll just have to take her word for it.

"What I don't understand is why this man is singing Cat's songs?"

"What do you mean?"

"Well, he is singing to the same melody but the words are all wrong. They are human words instead of cat words."

"Well, maybe Cat has used the melody of George Michael and made his own words to it?" I suggested and that was a big mistake. She started screaming and hollering so much so that the other cats came running in to see what was going on. "Is Mommy torturing you?" Jimmy was the first to arrive.

"No, I'm not Jimmy and that is not a funny thing to say."

"Well then what did you say?"

I explained to the others what had happened. Jimmy started mumbling about how I could be so stupid. Of course Cat did not steal the melody from some human singer. He would never stoop so low. "Some human singer?" I asked a bit annoyed. At that point Bear stepped in. He explained to Jimmy and Maya that many artists used materials from other artists. However they only did that because they admired the other artists so much. "Oh, so this human stole the melody from Cat!" was Maya's conclusion. Now it was my turn to laugh at their stupidity for once and asked Maya how long Cat had been in the music business. "Almost all his life" she responded "two and a half years. He started when he was only 6 months old." "Oh, so he is a kitten star?" I asked a bit sarcastically. She nodded greedily, not really getting the sarcastic part.

Bear explained once more that George Michael was in the music business for a long time already. "Mommy and Daddy have been listening to him as long as I can remember" he told Maya. She looked as if we had given her the worse news in the world. So I quickly added that it was not a bad thing to cover someone else's songs. "You must see it as homage to the other artist. One day other cat artists and perhaps human artists will cover songs written by Cat." This eased Maya's mind.

"I can go to his concert, right Mommy?" she asked.

"A concert?"

"Yes, there is going to be a concert by Cat in my nightclub" Bear said "but she wasn't supposed to know about that" he finished with an angry look in Maya's direction. Maya shrunk by the angry look of Bear. I asked Maya how she knew about the concert. She said she had overheard him making arrangements. Turns out that ever since Bear has saved her from Jimmy's pestering she is always as close to him as she can.

Jimmy is like a boy in third grade teasing the little girls from first grade. In this case, the girl he is teasing is Maya. I told Jimmy to stop doing it and it has become less, but every now and then he does it anyway. The last time that happened, Bear stepped in and showed Jimmy his place. Now every time Jimmy tries something she immediately starts screaming for Bear who then, very duly, shows up. All he has to do is show up to make Jimmy scurry away. Besides that she always makes sure she is very, very close to Bear. Whenever he's at work she sits in his office. Most often behind a cabinet or something because she knows Bear does not want to be disturbed at work.

So that is how she overheard Bear talking to the agent of Cat. And again she asked "I can go right Mommy?" I was hesitant "You're only 8 months old, I think that is a bit too young to go to a concert." "I'm 10 months!" she cried. I looked at Bear hoping on his input, but he was obviously not planning to make this easier for me. So I put my foot down and said I was not letting her go to this concert. "I'm not letting you go out so late at night" I said, hoping that was the last of it when Bear announced "there will also be a matinee performance in the afternoon". This made Maya bounce up and down "I'm going to Cat, I'm going to Cat!" I softly cursed Bear. Couldn't he have said that before? I asked Bear how security was going to be. He explained that there would be three matinee shows and he wasn't allowing more than 50 cats per show. For the night shows the amount was 75 cats per show. "Luke will be in charge of security, as usual" he ended.

"As usual?" I inquired.

"Oh, you don't know?"

"No, I don't. What is there to know?"

"Luke is my bouncer in the nightclub."

"I thought he was your bartender?"

"That too, but he also makes sure there are no fights."

"Are you sure about that, Bear?" I asked very carefully.

"Yeah, why?"

"Well, Luke is very likely to be the one to start the fight."

"Oh no, Mommy" Bear giggled "he's past that now.'

"Not for nothing, Bear, but three months ago he hurt his leg in a big fight, remember."

"That was three months ago. He doesn't do that anymore."

"Well if you say so."

I am so glad that with Bear I can at least have a normal conversation (if that is a word you can even use). So I demanded to know how Luke was planning on doing security. Maya was already on her way to get Luke even before I finished my sentence and shortly after he came walking in. As I saw him strolling in I must say he is a sight. He has grown into a huge cat. Big and strong with that cool, tranquil Sylvester Stallone look. I could see why Bear asked him to be bouncer at his club. You would have to have a lot of guts to take it up against him. I think the club is very safe right now. "What?" Luke asked gruffly when he reached me. "How are you planning on taking care of safety during the concert of Cat?" Luke sighed, obviously annoyed by the fact that I was asking "there will only be 50 kittens during each matinee so I thought I would handle that myself."

"Have you ever seen 50 kittens? Female kittens, I might add, at a concert?" "No, but how hard can it be?"

"Well, imagine 50 kittens like Maya, yelling and screaming and fainting and scratching each other to get close to the stage."

"Oh, don't be ridiculous, Mommy. Cats don't do that."

"Don't they? Maya?" I looked at Maya and asked "What are you going to do as soon as Cat gets on stage?"

"Oh, at first I will probably faint at the beautiful sight of his presence and after that I will probably hit everybody in sight who even gets close to him." I looked at Luke who was staring at Maya in shock. "You have some safety precautions to take, my dear." He mumbled "holy crap" and he was off. Bear was right behind him yelling that he would like to keep the club in one piece.

"So I can go then, Mommy" Maya stated.

"I don't think so, dear" I replied which sent her into one of her fits again. To appease her I told her that as soon as Luke had his security measures in place I would like to hear them. Then I would see how the first show goes and if I was pleased with the results, she could go to the last show. "But I want to go to every show!" she cried. "And how are you going to pay that entrance fee three times?" I asked. "Bear will let me in for free, he promised me." I sighed heavily. None of the boys gave me this much trouble. I told her that she could go the two last shows if I was satisfied with Luke's security. She was still not pleased and mumbled something that sounded like "we'll just see about that..." and quickly left the room. I tell you, raising your cats to become honorable members of the cat society is not an easy task.

11.
The concert

For the next few days I saw Bear and Luke having little meetings during the day. Obviously Luke was a bit upset about what was awaiting him. At night I saw them in the back of the yard in a deep discussion with some other tomcats. Big, bulky tom cats I may add.

On Wednesday (the first concert was planned on Friday) Luke came up to me and sat next to me on the couch. "What's the matter, dear? You look tired" I said as I stroked him on his head. He gave a deep and heavy sigh but said nothing. Obviously he was just looking for some rest and some comfort. He laid next to me after a while and fell asleep. Poor thing, he has been working so hard. After Luke had been sleeping for about ten minutes, Maya came running in. She jumped on Luke and started asking him if everything was in order for the concert. Luke was very annoyed at the fact that his rest was disturbed so I grabbed Maya to keep him from hitting her. "Would you like to go and sleep in our bedroom for a while, Luke?" I asked while still holding Maya. He did not answer but just walked to our bedroom. I let him in and watched him as he dropped on our bed and immediately fell asleep. All the while Maya was kicking and screaming in my arms, crying that she wanted to go to the concert.

I calmed her down by saying there was nothing to worry about and that I was sure Luke had the security measures all taken care of in such a way that I was going to let her go to the concert. She was ecstatic and cried "Oh yes, please Mommy, I have to hear Cat sing Careless Whiskers life!" I could not help myself but I burst out in laughing, which of course was the worst thing I could have done. She struggled free from my arms and walked out of the room really offended.

I know I shouldn't have laughed but these cats are not very original. Maya was sitting with me the other day, showing me all her cosmetic products. She has special whiskers mascara of the brand Cover Cat. Her perfume is from Tommy Hillcat and the conditioner is from Herbal Cats. "You cats are not very original, are you?" I asked when I saw all the products displayed in front of me. "What do you mean?" she asked in her cutest voice.

"Oh, I don't know. Let me guess there is probably also a Cat Boss, Cat Secret and Cat Dior."

She scoffed at me and said "of course those are not real brand names. Don't be ridiculous"

"Well then, name a couple of the most famous brands in the cat world" I said. She thought for a while and said "well of course there is Elizabeth Cat, Christian Cat and lets not forget Calvin Cat."

"No, let's not. But are you sure it's not Cat Klein?"

She shook her head at my total stupidity "You don't get us cats, do you Mommy" she said accusingly.

"No honey, I don't. Mommy is a big idiot." That seemed to please her.

But I digress. At the end of the day Luke had recuperated a bit and I asked him how security was coming along. He said it was great. He had found six other cats who were willing to help him maintain order during the matinee concerts and three of those would also be present at the night concerts. I must say I am proud of my Luke. Bear would oversee the security of Cat together with another cat and they asked Angel to be available if things got really out of hand "he does that in the nightclub anyway every night, so there is nothing special there. He just has to work a few more hours, which I'm sure he can do." Luke concluded.

"Angel?" I asked "What Angel?"

"You know, Angel, that fat dog of yours!" I was highly offended "Angel is NOT fat! He is just built a bit bigger than his brother" I defended my Angel. Luke just looked at me and smiled. Oh, who was I kidding? I have to admit Angel is a bit on the fat side. I don't understand why though, we feed him less than his brother and yet he is almost 10 kilos heavier. And they are about the same height. Angel is just wider. "What does Angel do in the nightclub?" I quickly changed the subject.

"Angel?" Luke said "Angel is the cook."

"Angel prepares cat food?"

"Yes, and he's very good at it, I may add."

"And what else does he do?"

"Well, when things get really out of hand he just shows his face and barks to stop any fighting that might be going on. He's highly effective in maintaining order." Luke continued telling me that the fighting has become less and less since Angel was employed by Bear "makes my job as bouncer a whole lot easier" he concluded. I must say that this revelation has given me some insight in the weight problem that Angel has. He probably tastes all his own cooking all night long.

"I think Maya will be glad to hear that she can go to the concert" I said to Luke. He sighed deeply "she has been a pain in the butt these last few days." I assured him that after I told her she could go to the concert she would not bother him anymore. "I sure hope so Mommy. She is a paw full."

I couldn't agree with him more and watched him leave for the club for more preparations. So I went in search for Maya to give her the good news.

I found her in front of my mirror in my bedroom. That explained the open door. As I walked in I saw her sitting on my dresser close to the mirror, with a little comb, making sure every hair was exactly in place. Now if you have cats you will know that their hair is always arranged perfectly. Especially if they are short haired cats. Long haired cats may need some brushing but short haired cats don't need that in order to look good. I always wondered how they do that and now I know.

She looked up from the mirror and looked at me in great expectation "Good news, Maya, you can go to the concert!" I said to her. She immediately jumped up and danced around the room while singing "I'm gonna see Cat, I'm gonna see Cat!" She finally turned to me and said "Oh, thank you Mommy, for letting me go to all the concerts."

"Who said anything about ALL the concerts? You can go to one concert" I told her.

"Oh, but that is no good, Mommy. Cat does something different every time, so I have to see all the concerts" she explained to me. Thinking I was smart I asked her where she was going to get the money to pay for the entrance fee for 6 concerts. She laughed and said "Bear is going to let me in for free, because I'm his little sister." I sighed; I should give up and not try to win from these cats. Trying to have the final word I told her she could only go to the afternoon concerts. This of course sent her into a hysteric fit, so I grabbed her by the scruff of her neck and held her up to face level. "Listen, to me Maya" I said very seriously "you are only going to the afternoon concerts. And if you don't promise me you will behave I will not let you go to any of the concerts." "Oh and how would you accomplish that?" She yelled at me. "I will simply ground you, starting Friday morning" I answered calmly.

"Well you can't lock me in a room all day."

"Oh, yes I can"

"Well, I won't come in Friday morning."

"Yes, you will, because you will be hungry and will want your breakfast."

"I'll ask Bear to bring me food."

"If you don't show up in the morning I will not feed any of them, see if they will be happy with that. Want to make a bet that the others will bring you to me within ten minutes?"

Maya sighed; she knew I was very serious and that she had no choice but to listen. However she is a cat and will never give in quietly. So after a few more minutes of threats from both sides she finally gave in.

I let her go and walked into the room in search for Bear and Luke. I gave them instructions not to let Maya in for the night concerts. They looked at each other and knew it was going to be tough. "The both of you are big cats, you should be able to handle a small kitty like Maya" I said. Bear sighed "Mommy, I can only promise you I will do everything in my power to stop her from getting in. However you know as well as I do that once she puts her mind to something, she is going to get it." "Yeah, what he said" Luke added. "Well, you better

do the best you can" I said "I'm counting on the both of you."
It's amazing that as the only female in the house, besides myself
of course, she had those males and those dogs, for that matter,
wrapped around her little paw.

We'll see what happens Friday.

12.
Missing

My cats get three meals per day. In the morning they get dry food, in the afternoon when I get home after work (around 5) they get a snack and then at around 10 or 11 in the evening they get their dinner, just before we head off to bed.

That Friday evening I came home a little after five in the afternoon. The cats were anxiously waiting for me. This is nothing unusual since they always do that when I come home in the afternoon. However when I grabbed the canister that contained the food, Bear jumped down from table and put his paw on the canister. "What?" I asked. "Can you give us dinner?" he asked while pointing to the cabinet containing the cans of wet cat food.

I looked at him in amazement. "We want our dinner now" Bear clarified. "Why?" was my logical question. "Because" was his simple reply. "Because doesn't do it for me, Bear. You'll have to give me more than that." He sighed "I would like to have dinner now, because we have a big evening ahead of us, with the concert starting in an hour. And at 11 the late night concert starts, so we don't have time for dinner then." "Is everybody going to the concert at 6?" I asked. More sighs at my complete ignorance, the answer was that only Maya was going to the 6 o'clock concert but the others were all going to the 11 o'clock concert but they had to be there at 10 for the opening act. Of course Luke and Bear would be busy with security at both concerts. "If I give you dinner now, can I come and see Cat perform?" I tried. A cry of protest arose from all the cats, which was the answer I was expecting. "Okay, I'll give in, but just for today!" I warned all of them as I proceeded to put the food in their dishes. Of course they did not listen to me and gobbled down their food as fast as they could.

Normally I see cats lying around the house all evening. That Friday however, not one cat in sight. They did not even come in later in the evening to ask for some more dinner, which I really was expecting. It must be a really good show that this Cat gives.

The next morning they were all sprawled out around the house in deep sleep. I tried waking them to find out how it all went, but to no avail. They didn't even come for their breakfast. I asked Angel how things went. He told me he left at one in the morning while the partying was still going on. "Was the concert over by then?" I wanted to know. "How should I know, I can't hear the difference" was his answer. I smiled and asked if he had to work again tonight. "I work every night, Mommy" he replied. "Good for you, Angel!"

Of course Maya was in seventh heaven. She had seen Cat and was even invited to his dressing room for the after concert party. She showed me his picture with paw print (cat version of an autograph) that he had given her. I offered to frame it for her but she refused and kept the picture close to her. "Can I go again tonight?" she asked in her sweetest voice. I did not see why not, so I told her she could. This made her ecstatic and she starting jumping up and down and telling every one she came across that she was going to Cat's concert again. Luke came walking in and heard it. He walked over to me and sternly asked me if I had gone mad. I was taken back a bit by that statement and asked him why he would say something like that. "That cat is crazy" he announced "yesterday she was a total pain in the butt. She acted like one spoiled kitten all through the concert." Apparently that was not all that she did. She was telling everybody all through the concert how she knew Luke and the owner of this great nightclub. She acted like one little diva. She did impress lots of cats there and she was now a little famous. This only made Luke's job harder because every time he tried to call her to order she called a few of her new found "friends" and they ganged up against Luke. So I went over to Maya and told her that if she showed any more of that behavior, I had authorized Luke to expel her from the concert. Furthermore I told her that she would definitely not be allowed to go to the final concert on Sunday if she kept it up. Last but not least I tried to explain to her that this was behavior unbecoming her upbringing and I was very disappointed in her. This seemed to get through to her and she promised to better her ways.

For the rest of the weekend things were quiet. Except for Bear and Luke who, of course, had to attend all the concerts, the others decided to stay home. Once was more than enough of that "pompous loud ugly singing cat", as Mozes called him. I think he's a bit jealous of all the female attention Cat gets.

On Sunday night or actually Monday morning early, there was a horrible thunderstorm. The concert was long over. The Sunday concert was at nine, so I was happy to see Luke and Bear inside. When I walked around the house to see if everybody else was inside, I came to the conclusion that Maya was not at home. I looked and looked, knowing how afraid she is of thunder and checked behind every couch, table and cabinet. Everywhere! I finally turned to Luke and asked if he had seen Maya. "No..." he said in a rather hesitant and strange way and started to walk away from me, rather slowly. "Luke, come back here" I admonished him "where is Maya?"

"She's at the after concert party with Cat" he finally said while he kept looking at his paws.

"What! What is she doing at that party?"

"She's been going to all of them, all weekend"

"Are you telling me she has been going to the night concerts as well as the matinee concerts?"

"Euuhhhh, yes. Didn't you know that?" Luke replied, trying to change the subject.

"You know very well I did not know that. Why did you let her in?"

"She's difficult" was the only statement I got out of him.

"Are you telling me you can't handle that kitten? You are three times her size and four times her weight."

"Have you ever felt those nails?" he cried and ran out of the room. What a hero!

So I turned to Bear who was also trying to get away before I saw him, as were all the others. "Bear, come back here" I cried, while another thunderclap crashed through the sky. "I don't know where she is, Mommy, honest I don't. This last after concert party was not at the club. I closed early tonight." He quickly said and went to hide under the table.

As I was standing on the front porch, watching the rain pour down, seeing the lightning and hearing the loud thunderclaps. I was terribly upset. This storm was directly above us and had no signs of stopping any time soon. In between the noise I tried calling out to Maya every now and then.

Finally after two hours of rain it started to subside a little and the down pour turned into a drizzle. I called Maya a couple of times again and finally saw something moving in the dark. It was Maya! I was ecstatic and ran inside to get a towel. She was on the porch by the time I got back with the towel.

"Oh, Maya, darling, I was so worried! I am so glad you are alright!" I sobbed. She let me dry her off and was obviously glad to be home. By the time I got her dry I wrapped her in another towel and held her close to me. "Where were you, Maya? I was worried sick!"

"I was with Cat, Mommy but on my way home it started to rain so I hid under a tree."

"What were you doing at Cats party, Maya? Didn't I tell you to come home after the concert?"

"Would you turn down an invitation from a famous star?" she asked me, thinking she was being smart.

"I would, if I knew it would get my mother upset" I countered.

"But if it hadn't started raining, I would have been home at a regular hour and you would never have known."

"So you do things I forbid you, just because you think I am not going to find out about it?"

She knew now that she was in a tight spot. I was still holding her in the towel and the anger in my voice was very obvious.

"Do you know what Cat called me?" she said trying to change the subject.

"I don't care, Maya." I was really angry with her now. Just because she's so darn cute she thinks she can get away with just about anything.

"He calls me gorgeous Maya" she tried again.

"That obviously only counts for the outside" I said deeply disappointed in her and I put her down. I walked away from her. I was just so upset and she thought it was all a big joke. Seeing how upset I was she ran after me and jumped on the kitchen counter to get closer to me.

"What's the matter Mommy?" she asked.

"You have to ask?"

"I'm home safe aren't I?"

"Do you have any idea how worried I was?"

"Why would you be so worried about me? I can take care of myself."

"That is the same thing Mickey said" I answered and walked away with tears in my eyes.

After I calmed down a little I came back out and closed up for the evening, gave the cats their food and turned out the lights. Maya walked behind me the entire time, but I ignored her. I wanted her to know I was angry with her. She finally couldn't take it anymore and ran to the bedroom door and wouldn't let me in until I acknowledged her. "Why are you so upset Mommy?"

"You really have to ask?"

"I know you are angry with me and that I am grounded, but there is something else going on."

"Yes, there is, I don't want you to end up the same way Mickey did."

"Oh, but I won't. I'm smart."

"So was Mickey!'

"He was?"

"Yes!" and I walked into the bedroom, leaving her outside, I did not want her to see me crying.

13.
Mickey

The next morning I continued to ignore Maya. I was still very upset with her. My husband told me that she had been asking him why I was so upset. He told her that she had broken our trust and that would take time to heal again. This did seem to get through to her a little because she was very demure the whole day.

That afternoon I was sitting outside when Maya walked up to me. She sat in front of me on the table, did not say a word but softly put her paw on my hand. I looked up at her and saw by the expression on her face that I got through to her. "Mommy" she said softly "who is Mickey?" I was silent for a moment thinking how I could describe Mickey.

Who is Mickey? Or rather who was Mickey? Mickey was the only cat of any pedigree that I ever had. His father was a price winning Cornish Rex and his mother was a regular European Shorthair. While his father was a beautiful golden brown and his mother was white with black and red spots, Mickey turned out silver grey. A Cornish Rex is a cat with curly hair. Mickey did not have curly hair. I always joked that he had a perm which had gone bad. There was some frizzle to his hair but it was mostly long. A friend of ours once described him as "the cat that stuck his paw into the electric outlet and exploded".

Mickey was a small cat, much smaller than all our regular big bulky cats. He was one of my favorites probably because he always wanted to be close to me. He felt safe whenever he was on my shoulder. Whenever he wanted to be carried he would sit in front of me and then jump up and I would have to catch him and drape him over my shoulder. He could spend hours there.

He would love to run. In our house in Holland we had two cat doors. One leading from the living room to the garage and the other from the garage leading outside. The yard was fenced and the cats could not get out of it. This gave me great peace of mind. It meant the cats could go in and out as they pleased without us having fear for them getting lost or worse. What Mickey would do is come in from the outside like the devil was on his tail. I would hear the cat door in the garage slamming and shortly after I would hear the other one, after which he would run up the stairs, to the bedroom door. Then he would turn by jumping up sideways, putting his paws on the door, pushing himself away and proceeding to do the whole route again, the other way. Like I said he was a small cat of only 6 pounds but when he did that it was like a herd of elephants coming by.

He had this "nice" habit of doing it in the middle of the night. It would scare the heck out of me. So almost every morning I would come down and tell Mickey that I did not think it was funny to scare me like that. He always said he was sorry, but I think he could just not help himself.

He just loved to run. Things would get really hectic when one of the others decided to join in the fun. That would get me out of bed and sometimes I believe that it was the only reason he (they) did it. Of course they always denied it, but I know better.

Because of his fluffy look Mickey resembled a little a plush animal and one time he had managed to sneak into our bedroom and crawled in between my plush animals which I had on our couch. We did not notice him at all, but in the middle of the night I woke up because he had sneaked into our bed and was happily sleeping in between us. I asked him how he had done that but he only smiled at me. So the next day he figured that this was the way. He sneaked into our bedroom once more, but this time he was so content with himself that he starting purring. You have cats that purr softly, but not so Mickey. It was like a generator was turned on. So we were in bed and the purring started. My husband turned on the light and looked around where this sound was coming from. We finally found him in between the plush animals. It was the perfect hiding place for him. So that is how he did it that night before! Too bad for Mickey he betrayed himself. Otherwise he could have done that trick for many more nights, before we would ever have found out where he was hiding.

Needless to say it did not happen anymore after that.

When we moved to Aruba we took our little devil with us together with the three brothers and he loved it here. His rather thick fur did not deter him from running around. Whenever I would take a walk in our garden (which is rather large) he would go with me and then wait all the way in the back until I was near the house again at which point he would come running past me at top speed. Did I mention that he just loved to run?

Mickey was a very intelligent cat. Most cats start talking at about 10 weeks (if they talk at all, but that's a totally different story). Mickey started babbling at six weeks, right after we got him and was speaking rather well at 8 weeks old already. Goofy gave him special tutoring at home and he was at the big cat school by the time he was 6 months. Normally that would be 9 months at the earliest. So he was gifted, but also spoiled. Okay I admit, that was my fault, but he was irresistible. "Just like me?" Maya asked. "Just like you" I said.

I was not going to explain that she was also irresistible in a completely different way. Not even sure that I could explain it. Mickey was just adorable even though he was a male. Maya is adorable but girl cats most often are adorable more easily then male cats. "So what happened to him?" Maya wanted to know.

Well besides that Mickey was really smart he was also rather arrogant. He knew best. I never knew what exactly happened, because I wasn't home when it happened but I can give it a pretty good guess. Mickey had found a way to get out of the yard and onto the terrain next to our house. There is no house there, but the neighbor's dogs next to that do roam that piece of land. I had told Mickey time and time again that he had to be careful, because those dogs were not like ours. They would not talk to him, like Angel and Nero do, but most likely hurt him. Mickey would always tell me that I worried too much. And obviously rightly so. One day I came home and he wasn't there waiting for me. He was always waiting for me, so I went in search for him.

We found him on the terrain next to our house; dead. I can only assume that those dogs I warned him about got him. I am horrified to think what happened that day. How he would not run away from them, thinking they would not harm him. I was devastated. I cried for two days and could not even work. Tears welled up as I told this to Maya and I could see she was touched by this as well.

We buried him in the yard, in a piece of cloth. My little Mickey. It is just so sad. These animals come into our lives and they steal a piece of your heart. When they die, they take that piece with them and your heart bleeds. Mickey did not take a little piece; he took a big chunk the day he died.

I stopped talking and looked at Maya.

"You still miss him, don't you Mommy?"

"Yes, I do, darling. Now do you understand why I was so upset yesterday? I don't want the same thing to happen to you. I couldn't bear losing you too!"

"I do Mommy, and I promise I will be careful. I hate those dragons anyway and try to stay away from them as much as possible."

"But there is also the cars, darling. They could also hit you. I really would like it if you did not leave the house that much."

I knew I was asking too much now. She loved going out, to parties, to her friends' house, shopping at the cat mall. Just like a regular teenager. She looked at me and said "I'll try,

Mommy." "It's all I'm asking for, dear" and I grabbed her and hugged her.

I told her to remind me to tell her the story one day of when Mickey had to go to the dentist. She giggled; the idea of a cat going to the dentist was of course ridiculous. But Mickey went to the dentist.

Yes, he was very special indeed.

14.
How it all began

I promised in the beginning I would tell you how "that day" came about, so here goes. It all started when we had Clubby about a year and a half. In hindsight I think it started much earlier, but I did not notice that. Strange things started happening.

When my phone bill started to be much higher then usual was when I first got suspicious. After that I got friends and family telling me that my cat was answering the phone. So I started calling my house at odd times of the day and indeed the phone would be picked up and I would hear a meow. When I would say something the connection would be broken and calling again only resulted in getting a busy tone. Being busy with so many things I did not really have a lot of time to investigate.

But the little things just kept adding up. Mail arriving that was not for us but with our address and more of such oddities. Clubby and Cindy were also acting strange. They would sit close together at the end of the living room as if they were whispering to each other. Of course that was ridiculous, so I shook the feeling off.

Now we had a fairly regular schedule during the week, so we would always be home around the same time, until that one day. One of my classes was cancelled so I went home. Instead of coming home way after 5 in the afternoon, I came home a little after one. I will never know why, but when I approached my house I got this funny feeling. So I walked up to the door real slow and very softly opened the door.

The door from the hallway to the living room was a little open and I could hear a voice coming from the living room. My heart was thumping in my throat. Someone was in my house! I closed the front door as softly as I could and I stood at the other door listening to what was being said inside. I could hear someone speaking and then it would be silent, and an answer would come. This burglar had some nerve talking on my phone! However as I stood there I noticed that this was really odd. The voice was strange and why would someone break into my house just to use my phone? So I opened the door very slowly and looked inside the living room, to the spot where we had our phone.

I will never forget what I saw at that moment. There was Clubby sitting on the table next to the phone which was off the hook and he was talking into it and then putting his ear to the other side to hear what the person at the other end of the line was saying. Or was that a cat as well? I just stood there watching. A talking cat! His voice was a little high and a bit odd, but very clear and I understood every word. I don't know how long I stood there watching, but at a certain point I dropped my house keys, that had been dangling in my hand. The noise startled not only me but also Clubby and Cindy (who had been sitting on the couch).

Clubby tried to act as if I had seen and heard nothing and casually put his paw on the receiver and disconnected the phone conversation he was having. Cindy panicked and ran past me and ran upstairs. I don't know where she went and at that point I had no idea that she could talk as well. I just kept my eyes on Clubby because I was afraid that if I looked away it would turn out to have been a dream. Looking straight at him, I slowly started walking towards him and I softly heard him say "oh shit". Very clearly in an "I'm busted" tone.

Clubby did not go anywhere but just sat there as I approached. When I got close to him I grabbed him and held him in front of me and looked at him very intently. "Can you say something else?" I asked him still holding him in front of me. All that came out was a squeaky sound. Apparently I was squeezing him a bit too much, so I put him down on the table and sat on the couch myself. "Can you speak?" I tried again, convinced that I was dreaming. I will never forget those first words he said to me. Clubby looked me in the eye and said in a loud and clear (be it a little high) voice "Yes." Obviously he figured there was no sense in denying it. I dropped back into the couch and ran my hands over my face. This was just too much! A talking cat! "but...how? why, how... when..." I was stammering. He giggled a little and said "surprise!" Well, he got that right!

I just sat there staring at this black and white animal sitting very casually on the salon table. "Maybe you should get us both something to drink and I'll explain everything" Clubby said after a few minutes. Since I was still in dumbfounded mode I got up and poured the both of us some milk. I sat at the kitchen table and he sat on the kitchen table with his milk in a saucer.

Clubby lapped his milk a little then sat back and looked at me "so, what would you like to know?"

Well I was thinking "how about everything" but started with the question "do all cats talk?"

"No."

"Does Cindy talk?"

"Yes."

"Have you been talking all your life?"

"Yes."

"Is there also something like a cat language?"

"Yes."

"Are there other people that know about this?"

"No."

Needless to say I was getting totally frustrated by his answers.

"Oh, for crying out loud Clubby, can you say anything other than 'yes' and 'no'?"

"Sure." (Heavy sigh)

At that moment my husband walked in, also a lot earlier than normal. It was a strange day indeed. He asked me what I was doing. I said nothing but turned to Clubby. He knew he would never be able to keep this from my husband so he turned to him and said "hello!" My husband dropped everything he was holding and stumbled back, falling into the kitchen cabinets, mouth open in disbelief. If I wasn't still in shock I would have found it hilarious. I have never seen a human being turn such a color pale. He managed to remain on his feet, staggered to the kitchen table and sat down as well.

So there we were, both staring at our cat. Clubby started explaining how cats indeed talk, but humans don't know this. Except for us two of course. Cats have their own schools, their own bars, massage salons, well you name it, they have it. They keep up appearances among humans because it's convenient that we give them food and shelter. Not all cats can talk human, but they also have their own cat language. Of course not all cats go to the schools and bars and such, because they don't want to. And sometimes they are kept inside by their humans.

What became clear in his "confession" is that cats almost always know exactly what you are saying and what you want them to do or in most cases, don't do. The only problem is that they just don't care. Humans are there to take care of the cats and the cats are not there to please the humans. "If you want that you should get yourself a dog" Clubby said prophetically. As for himself, it turned out that Clubby had a thriving little business. But unfortunately up to this day I still do not understand exactly what it is that he did. But I do know that he used our phone and our address to conduct his business which explained the high phone bills and the strange packages delivered to our house. And the name made sense as well: Mr. von Cathausen. Oh, he is a clever one.

After sitting there listening to this illuminating narrative, the only thing my husband could think of saying was "you know how to use a phone?" Clubby's eyes opened wide and he

SANDRA KLEIN

said "I bring you world shocking news and all you can ask is if I know how to use a phone?" "Well Clubby" I said "you must understand that we are in complete shock"

"I understand, and that is exactly the reason why you never should have found out about it."

"So what are we going to do about it?"

"Of course you cannot tell a soul about it."

"Who would believe us?"

I asked him if he could call Cindy so that we could hear her speak as well. So he jumped off the table, walked to the hallway and gave a strange meow. Within seconds Cindy was downstairs. They sat together for a while whispering to each other. The same way I had seen them do before, but now I knew what was going on. As the conversation was obviously coming to an end I saw Cindy nodding her head, when finally she walked up to the both of us and said "Hello!" It was the cutest and sweetest voice I had ever heard. So I picked her up and held her in my arms. "What a beautiful voice you have, Cindy!"

"Oh, why thank you ma'am."

My husband could only agree and as he stroked her he also praised her lovely voice. She giggled shyly and said "thank you, Sir".

"You know" Clubby said "maybe this is a good thing."

"How so, Clubby?"

"Now we can just tell you guys what we want and there will be no chance that you misunderstand us." My husband and I looked at each other. I wasn't so sure if it was indeed a good thing. But on the other hand, how bad could it be? "It

84

may be a good thing indeed, Clubby, but you guys have to stop calling us ma'am and sir." Cindy, whom I was still holding in my arms, looked up at me and said "can I call you Mommy and Daddy?" I liked the sound of that, so we agreed that we would be Mommy and Daddy. So now you know what happened on "that day" sixteen years ago. Many cats have come and gone. Many cats will still come and go. We feel special that we have this secret knowledge about the cat world. Clubby explained to me that as long as we have cats who talk to us, when we bring in new ones, it will continue. "They will not know any better" is what he always used to say. However if for some reason all our "talking" cats are gone and we get new ones, they will never talk to us. Guess we will have to make sure there is always one talking cat around.

It does make life a little easier. But they do have their nasty little habits. And with that I mean ignoring you and using you when it is convenient for them. After all they are still cats. At times I would ask one of them something and they would ignore me. I would then proceed to pick them up, and hold them in front of me, so they couldn't ignore me. The standard answer was always "I did not feel like answering you."

In the beginning it was hard. We would treat them like humans which they are definitely not. It's an easy mistake to make, since they talk and everything. But we've managed to get through it and now we just let them be cats and they let us be humans. It works out just fine.

Before I started this book I made sure a message got to Clubby via Goofy. Goofy and Clubby still send each other messages on a regular basis. I wanted to know if he would be okay with me writing this book. The answer? "Go right ahead, no one will believe you anyway!" Thanks Clubby.

I miss talking to Clubby. Wish I could pick up a phone and call him, but unfortunately that is not an option.

15.
Short Stories

There are a lot of stories and anecdotes that I can tell about my cats but they do not fill an entire chapter. That is why I decided to collect the most memorable ones in this chapter.

While looking at little Max at 3 months old and wondering why he is not speaking yet. I turn to Clubby:

"You think something is wrong with Max?"

"Why?"

"Because he's not talking and he is already three months old."

"Oh no, there is nothing wrong with him. He's just stupid."

Listening to Goofy and Aristotle having a conversation on the front porch:

Aristotle: "Can you lick me?"

Goofy: "Why?"

Aristotle: "Because I am too lazy to lick myself."

Luke and Mozes in the back yard looking at the huge amounts of water (due to heavy rain fall) flowing through our garden:

Luke: "You think they will notice?"

Mozes: "Notice what?"

Clubby looking on while my husband is fixing his motorcycle:

"Do you have any idea what you're doing?"

"I do."

"Are you sure?"

"Yes."

"Then where is the third wheel?"

"This motor cycle only has two wheels?"

"And you ride on it?"

"Yes."

"You're kidding me right?"

"No, I'm not."

"Well then show me."

"I can't, it's not working right now."

"I rest my case."

After I put some medicinal cream on Aristotle's paw he walked up to his brother.

Ari: "Lick my paw!"

Goofy: "Why don't you do it yourself?"

Ari: "Because this stuff Mommy put on it is gross!"

Goofy: "Then do it yourself."

Ari: "I'll pay you one dollar."
Goofy: "Okay."

At night before going to bed I like to enjoy a glass of milk. Of course whenever I pour myself a glass, the cats in the vicinity also want some, which they usually get. This night however I did not have regular milk but something called milk & fruit. It's quite tasteful and refreshing, for humans that is. Cats hate it. Mozes had never seen or tasted that particular product so he was sitting on the kitchen island, watching me pour myself a glass.

Mozes: "Give me some"
Me: "You don't like this."
Mozes: "Yes, I will. Give me."
Me: "Okay, but don't say I did not warn you."

I pour a little in his bowl and he takes one lick of the fluid, after which he sits straight up.

Mozes: "Are you trying to poison me or something? That is just gross!"
Me: "Didn't I tell you?"
Mozes: "You said I wasn't going to like it, not that it's pure poison."
Me: "Aren't we exaggerating just a little here?"
Mozes: "Cats never exaggerate!" and he walked away.

Luke: "My name is Juke."
Me: "No, it's Luke."
Luke: "Juke!"

Me: "Repeat after me."

Luke: "Repeat after me."

Me: sigh "Lion."

Luke: sigh "Lion."

Me: "Landing."

Luke: "Landing."

Me: "Luke."

Luke: "Juke."

Me: "No, Lllluke."

Luke: "No, Jjjjuke."

Me: "Never mind darling. Why don't you go play outside?" I pick him up and put him on the floor. At that moment Mozes walks in and they walk to the back door together.

Mozes: "So what have you and Mommy been talking about?"

Luke: "For some reason Mommy wants me to say that my name is Juke instead of Luke."

Mozes: "Humans are just plain weird!"

Luke: "Tell me about it."

Trying to convince Luke that he should not fight with all the cats in the neighborhood we had the following conversation.

Me: "Why do you do it Luke? Does he come into the yard?"

Luke: "No, he sits on the wall and shouts obscenities to Maya. So as the alpha male I have to kick his butt."

Me: "What kind of obscenities does he shout?"

Luke: "He says things like, "hey good looking, wanna go out", and stuff like that."

Me: "Haven't you ever heard of the saying sticks and stones can break my bones, but words will never hurt me?"

Luke: "Have you ever heard that offense is the best defense?"

Me: "Turn the other cheek?"

Luke: "Never trust the enemy!"

Me: "Love thy neighbor?"

Luke: "Kill the enemy! KILL! KILL!"

Me: "Maybe you should cool off in the bedroom for a while dear."

"Mommy, mommy, come quick!" Mozes shouts as he comes running into the living room. "What is it, dear?" "Come, come" he says as he walks outside and I follow. He leads me to the remains of a lizard. "Tadaah!"

"That's what you wanted to show me?"

"It is the first lizard I caught!" he says proudly.

"You are two years old and this is the first time you caught a lizard all by yourself?"

"Yes" he said proud, oblivious to my sarcasm "it's for you."

"Well thank you Mo, but I don't want it."

"You don't?"

"Not really, no."

"Aren't you proud of me?"

"I'm very proud of you; I just don't want a dead lizard."

"Why not?"

"Because it's gross!"

"They are delicious!"

SANDRA KLEIN

"You eat it."
"Okay."

Every now and then I feed my cats fresh fish. I get a few kilo's of whiting, boil them till they are soft, then clean them and divide among the cats. I really don't like to do it, because it's a lot of work and the whole house smells like fish for three days. So maybe twice a year they get this delicacy. Mickey was about 9 months old when I prepared whiting for the first time with him around. All the cats went crazy and Mickey being the youngest and not knowing what was going on went along with the frenzy. All the others were telling him how delicious it was. "Fresh fish...hmmmmm" Clubby said and asked me for the gazillionth time if it was ready.

The "moment supreme" finally arrived and I gave everyone their dish with fresh whiting. They all attacked and little Mickey expecting the most wonderful dish in his entire life, jumped at his dish. He smelled the fish, took one little bite and spewed it all out. Disappointed he looked from his dish to that of the others who were all eating like they hadn't been fed in ten days. He once again looked at his dish and gave it another try but could just not get himself to eat it. I was standing there feeling really sorry for the little one. He was so hoping for the meal of a lifetime.

Very disappointed he looked up at me and said "I don't like this Mommy." I picked him up "but it's fish, honey, all cats love to eat fish" and I looked down at Clubby who was finishing off Mickey's dish. "I hate it" little Mickey said, very sad. I really think he was on the verge of crying. "What would you like to eat then, dear? I'll get you anything you want" I tried to cheer him up. "Can I have some cheese?" he asked looking a little better.

"Of course you can have some cheese" and I walked to the kitchen. I put him on the table and got the cheese. I gave him some extra cheese that day. Mickey never ate anything with fish and preferred cheese above anything else. He was just plain weird, but I loved him so much.

I already mentioned that the cats are fed their last meal in the evening before we go to bed. They are not always all at home so I usually call out to them while locking up for the night. They always come running, but there was one night when Mozes did not show up. I called and called but finally decided that he would have to go without dinner that night. A little after midnight I was awakened by soft scratching on the bedroom door and a soft voice calling "Mommy! Mommy!" I got out of bed and opened the door. In front of the bedroom door there was Mozes sitting. "Mommy" he whispered "you forgot to feed us."

"No, Mo, everybody else ate but you didn't come when I called you."

"I never heard you calling!" he proclaimed indignantly.

"Well I did and you didn't come" I said while I closed the door to the bedroom. We were now standing in the hallway and I was really sleepy.

"Anyway, I'm here now. Can I have dinner now?"

"No, Mo, you can't."

"What do you mean: no?

"I mean: no, you can't have dinner."

"What a ridiculous answer that is. Of course I can have dinner now."

"You should have been here when I gave dinner to everyone else. Maybe this will teach you to listen more carefully when I call."

He snickered softly, looked up to me and said "You truly believe that Mommy?"

And he was right. What was I thinking? As if this would really teach him (or any of the other cats for that matter) anything. I shook my head and said "it was worth a try anyway" and proceeded to walk to the kitchen. Mo jumped on the kitchen island and before he started eating he looked at me and said "I must commend you on your effort Mommy, but you know it's useless" and proceeded to eat his food.

16.
Katinka

Sometimes people say to me that it would be nice if their animals could talk to them. I just smile and think to myself "if only they knew." While I see the benefits of it at times, I am mostly not very happy about that day I walked in on Clubby. They have a warped sense of humor and a very warped logic. It wears you out. The previous chapter is a good example of what I am talking about.

However it is not all bad. Some of the things that have happened in those years are precious. One of those things is little Katinka or Pookie as I nicknamed her. Pookie was found on a field that surrounded the company I worked at. She was the only kitten in a litter and as soon as we got the opportunity a colleague and I snatched her. No way was she going to survive in the wild.

I took her home and this picture was taken two days after she came to our house. Isn't she just a doll?

Unfortunately there was something wrong with Pookie. Turned out she was blind. We never found out if she could see just a little, like shadows and a little light and dark. At times we thought she did, but at other times we concluded that she had to be completely blind. But she was extremely intelligent!

Goofy, being used to working with kittens, took her under his wings when we got her. I will never forget those first weeks when he would take her by the paw, and walk through the house. He would stop at every obstacle and tell her what it was. He also made her feel it.

It is then that I found out the functionality of cat whiskers. It was amazing to see how she would walk very thoughtfully through the house and when she passed something really close you would see her correcting her course just a little, simply because the points of her whiskers brushed against a chair leg, or something else. It was only at times that she would walk straight toward a table leg that she would bump into it. Of course something like that startled her and she would sit and rub her paw over her nose. We tried not to laugh when that happened.

If she wanted to jump onto something, she would first feel with her paws how high it was and then jump. Of course she only did this when she was bigger, because as a six week old kitten she could not reach anything, except for Goofy's belly.

I always love having a new kitten in the house. They are so innocent and they have so much to learn. They do not yet see the dangers and they will jump and fall and learn. I love to sit and watch them as they explore the house. With Pookie it was a little different. Goofy would take her to a certain part of the house and he would tell her exactly where she was and what was standing where.

I remember sitting watching the two of them. It was priceless. "Now Katinka, today we are standing in front of the music cabinet of Mommy and Daddy. It begins here…" and he led her to one side of the cabinet "and ends here…" and he walked her to the other side. Our "music" cabinet as Goofy called it was an open cabinet with shelves on which we had our CD's. On top we had our television and the stereo, the next shelf held our video recorder with some videos and then two shelves with CD's. "These are the boxes in which they keep their music…." and he put her little paw on the CD boxes. Not being able to talk really well yet, Katinka looked up and said "music wox?" "Yes" Goofy explained "in these boxes they keep shiny discs which they put in that machine there" as he pointed to the stereo on top of the cabinet. "They press a button and music comes out." Katinka tried to act as if she understood everything but it was obvious that she didn't and finally she said "discs?" "Yes, I guess you could compare it to our CD's but humans are not as smart as we are in those things."

I know, I know, I should have objected and put him straight at that moment. However I just let it be. I mean Goofy wasn't obviously that bright himself, pointing to things while he knew she couldn't see anything. And so it was for the next few weeks; Goofy teaching little Katinka all there was to know about the house. He must have been a very good teacher because she could find her way about the house like no other. She would run around, play with a cat toy with a bell. That was so much fun. She would run after the toy when I threw it away and she would always know exactly where it was.

Sometimes she would play with Goofy. They would run after each other and as soon as Goofy got tired of playing he would sneak away very silently. Poor little Katinka would stop on the spot where she had heard Goofy last. You know, cats are supposed to be these elegant creatures that can walk through a room without being heard. It always seems as if mine can't. When they come running into the room it sounds as if a herd of elephants is approaching. I did notice a few times that they indeed can be silent if they benefit from it. I first saw it when Goofy and Katinka were playing. Goofy would come running in like a bunch of wildebeests but once inside he would stop and sneak away. Katinka running behind him would run until that very spot where Goofy stopped before he snuck off and look around and wonder where he had gone. Knowing I was in the room she would ask "Mommy, where did Goofy go?"

"He went upstairs darling."

"Why is he always hiding from me?"

"Isn't that what you guys are playing? Hide and seek?"

"Not really."

"Oh well, anyway, he's upstairs now."

And off she went to look for him. "Goofy! Goofy!" I would hear her call out in the hallway. A few seconds later Goofy would come running by on his way out, with just enough time to yell "I'm gonna get you for that!" while passing by. Katinka would follow him outside. But this time he would hide somewhere in the garden and she could not find him. Then she would come to me and explain that Goofy was not playing fair and then she always vowed never to play with him ever again.

A cat vowing to do or not do something doesn't mean a whole lot. The next day they would be playing again. As she grew older she depended less and less on Goofy to help her. She would ask me and she would get very upset if a piece of furniture had been moved. "Okay, who moved the chair?" is what I would hear every time she wanted to sleep on her favorite chair.

She did not go to cat school like all my other cats, because the school does not provide special teaching. She got a lot of her lessons from Goofy and from me. I would sit hours with her telling her about birds and mice. Goofy interrupted our lessons at every chance he got, saying I was doing it all wrong. I was teaching her too much human stuff according to him. So I moved our lessons to a time when Goofy was not at home. It resulted in me becoming very attached to little Katinka.

She was always around me and when I was sitting in the garden she would be near me or on my lap and we would talk. She was always chattering about what she wanted to be when she grew up. Of course she knew it would never be possible but we both just pretended. It was fun. When Katinka was four she started to get sick. She started acting funny and became paranoid. She would start hitting Goofy whenever he came close to her. I tried talking to the cats to not hit her back, because she was sick, but apart from Clubby, none of them understood what was going on. Cats will be cats. I think her other senses got bad as well, because she started to bump into furniture and walls but also into other cats. They would always slap her for doing that. That of course scared her and she would try to run away, but then she would bump into the next thing or cat and she would panic.

I tried to be around as much as possible and told her to sleep as much as possible whenever I wasn't around. Then when I was at home I would be able to help her. That worked fine for a while, but I saw she was getting worse. The doctors could not find anything wrong with her. After a couple of months she started to become aggressive. She did not recognize any of the cats anymore and started hissing and attacking them when she bumped into any of them. At a certain point she did not even recognize my husband anymore and was scratching him every opportunity she got. I was the only one who could handle her a little, but I saw that it was getting more and more difficult every day.

So I took her to the doctor once again. That was a nightmare. Because she was so aggressive she did not want anybody near her. I tried to comfort her, but she had gone paranoid. I finally managed to get her a little sedated with a little pill in her food. Boy, did I feel like a betrayer. When she was a little calmer I managed to get her to the vet. I was holding her tight in my arms and my voice did seem to calm her down a little. We found out that she had a tumor in her brain. Operation was impossible and because she could not live like this anymore, we decided to put her to sleep.

I held her all through it and did not let go until she was peacefully at sleep. It was the best thing to do, but it is always hard. Even harder when they are almost little human beings. When we came home I sat on the couch and just cried. Clubby came over and asked me what was wrong. So I told him. He looked at me and said "want me to tell you a little secret?"

"Sure..." while I sobbed heavily.

"You know that myth that you humans have about cats having 9 lives?"

"Yeah"

"It's not a myth."

"It's not?"

"No cats indeed have 9 lives. Every time we die we come back as another cat. Sometimes it takes just a few weeks before we come back but sometimes we return after a few months or even years."

"But you don't remember your former life do you?"

"No, we don't but we do get to choose our humans the second time around and each time after that."

"So, what are you saying?"

"The first time a cat is born into this world they are almost always born in rather bad situations. Faith will determine what will happen to them the first time around. We might spend our time on the street, or in the wild, or we may be lucky and get taken in by humans just like you and Daddy who take good care of us."

I looked at Clubby through my tears. Till now I was not really comforted for the loss of Katinka. He sighed in his typical "humans are stupid" sigh and continued to explain.

"When we pass on and we had a good life with certain humans we always try to get back to those humans in our next life. That is why we will sometimes wait for years before coming back as soon as the opportunity presents itself." At this point things started to get a little clearer.

"We could come back with another fur color or even as another race, but we will come back to you, if we liked it here. Pookie had a great life with you and I am convinced that she will return to you in another cat." I smiled through my tears and indeed felt a little comforted.

"But how will you know what cat ends up with what human?" Clubby smiled his mysterious smile and all he said was "we just know."

I was missing Katinka enormously but his words did comfort me a little. They also got me thinking, so the next day I sat down with Clubby to ask some more questions about this.

"Do cats know in which life they are?"

"Some do, some don't. Depends on how smart they are. Some cats choose not to learn from earlier lives and remain stupid throughout all nine lives. Others, like me, do learn and get smarter each time around."

"So in which life are you now?"

"I am at number six."

"Did you choose to live with us?" He smiled mysteriously once again but finally nodded his head. I smiled, I could not believe that we were "chosen" ones. I did not ask him on what he based his decision; I knew he would not answer me.

So that is the story of Katinka. I sometimes think she indeed came back as Maya. I have a very special bond with Maya and Maya is a little like the cat Katinka always said she wanted to be. It would not surprise me if she was.

17.
The Dentist

When will Luke ever learn? Once again he had been fighting and now his paw hurts again. Fighting with some cat because they said some nasty things about Maya, and because she lives in the same house it is his duty to protect her honor. I don't really understand why he feels he has to do that, especially since he is still angry with her about the whole concert incident. Whatever the case, the result is still one cat with a paw he can't walk on.

Now instead of just telling me that he wants to sleep in our bedroom because he feels sorry for himself, he decided to approach it differently. I was standing in the kitchen when all of a sudden I heard a pitiful cry from the hallway. I ran to see what was going on only to find Luke sitting in front of the bedroom door. "Have you gone out of your mind? I asked angrily and he said he needed to get my attention, because he wanted to sleep on our bed. I told him that he could have asked when he was with me in the kitchen two minutes ago and that I would even have carried him. "But the doctor told me to do it like this" he said meekly, so I opened the door and let him into the bedroom. "Your doctor is an idiot" I told him while I closed the door. My husband walked into the hallway and asked what was going on. "Cat doctor" was the only thing

I said and he nodded understandingly. "Remember Mickey?" he said. I sure did remember Mickey and the time he went to his doctor and came home with a note.

But before I go into that perhaps I should explain something first. Cats have their own doctors. They are not trained in any medical way like human doctors, but they do serve a purpose. Or at least that is what I am told. I highly doubt the functionality of these cat doctors, but who am I to argue? Anyway, a cat doctor does not do any medical diagnosis. What he does is tell cats how they can get the attention of their owners in the best way. Of course it has to be in a way in which it becomes clear what is wrong with the cat. So with Luke for example he needs a comfortable place to sleep so his paw can rest. He then proceeds to scream in front of the bedroom door, because there he's most comfortable and all the while he is limping more thea he has to and constantly keeps his paw in front of him.

The cat doctor (or is it the doctor cat?), gives these instructions to cats. For a tummy ache he will "prescribe" eating grass and then vomiting on your owner's best chair, carpet or sofa. If that doesn't get their attention, you should do the same procedure again but during dinner time, near, or preferably on the dinner table. Then the owners will know that the cat has a stomach problem and take the animal to the veterinarian. Of course you would think that every cat can think that up all by himself, but apparently some of them need coaching.

In Mickey's case it was a bit different. Now all this happened when we were still living in Holland. He was one year old, if I remember correctly, when he had a little bit of a tooth problem. His upper left canine tooth was growing a little crooked. This caused the tooth to stab his lower jaw whenever he closed his mouth. Eating was a bit difficult as was closing his mouth. Furthermore the upper tooth was pushing his lower corner tooth out. Instead of coming to me with his problem he went to the cat doctor. I can only imagine the fancy ways the doctor thought up to get my attention, but Mickey told him that he could talk to me. I don't know if the cat doctor was in shock about that fact, but he did write me a note. In cat language...

Now you probably never saw a note in cat language. I can tell you it was my first time as well. Cat writing is more like claw markings with ink. Unfortunately I lost the note, otherwise I would have showed it to you, so let me describe it. There were cat claw markings on the paper, made with ink. Sometimes it was 2 nails, or 1 or 4 and they all were dragged down a little at different angles and lengths; sometimes in a swirl and sometimes making a sharp hook. At the bottom of the page there was a full paw print. I assumed that was the doctor's signature.

I was sitting on the couch when Mickey brought me the note. I unfolded it and looked at it. "What's this honey?" I asked while I looked at him next to me on the couch. "A note from my doctor" he explained.

"Do you mind telling me what it says?"

"Oh, oops, sorry, forgot you can't read cat" he said as he moved closer to read the note. "Okay" he started "it says" and he took a deep breath "Miw, meow meow mew. Miw miw miauw meeew miauw. Mew mew miauw meeew meew maw. Miew" after which he sat back and looked at me. He was so proud that he had read the entire note without hesitating or faltering. I just sat there with the note in my hand looking at him questioningly. Of course I understood nothing of the entire note, but that fact wasn't getting through to little Mickey. He kept looking at me in anticipation of what I was going to say now. Finally I said "darling?"

"Yes, Mommy?"

"Could you translate for me?"

"Translate?"

"Yes, translate. What does miw mean?"

"Oh no, you are saying it all wrong. It's more like mmiww."

"Okay then, what does mmiww mean?"

"You're not saying it quite right yet, Mommy. Try to let it come out of your throat more instead of your tongue."

"Mickey!" I cried impatiently "just tell me what the darn note says".

"Oh, well why didn't you just say so?" he replied smartly. I sighed and looked at him intently. He knew playing time was over now "it says I have to go to the dentist."

"Why?"

"Because my tooth is crooked."

"Let me see" and he showed me. "Ah yes, indeed darling. Guess we have to go to the vet."

"The vet? I have to go to the dentist!" Mickey protested.

"Yes, I know, but you don't think that we have special cat dentists, do you?" By the look on his face I knew that he did think that there were cat dentists.

"Let's just go to the vet and see what he says, okay?"

"Will you lock me in a cage?"

"Mickey, you've been to the vet before. To get your shots, remember? Did I put you in a cage then?"

"Oh, was that a vet?"

"Yes."

"That wasn't too bad. I think I can survive that…" he said happily and ran off to tell the others the news.

And so we went to the vet. Turns out he had to go to a specialist. We got all the paperwork from him. In the car Mickey started chanting 'I'm going to the dentist, I'm going to the dentist…" I wasn't going to tell him that going to the dentist isn't necessarily a fun thing to do.

I just drove home, called the specialist and set a date. Mickey was a pain in the neck all week. But finally the day was there. He did not want to go in the cat cage so as always he sat on the top of the back of the seat next to me. The trip from our home to Utrecht took about one hour. It must have been a strange sight for the cars passing us. Me with my cat sitting with his back side on the back of the seat, front paws on my shoulder and staring through the front window all the way. He could barely contain himself the whole trip.

When we arrived I hoisted the little one on my shoulder and went inside. The veterinary department at the University of Utrecht in Holland is highly specialized. They treat everything from cats and dogs to cows and horses. Before we went inside I told Mickey that he had to behave and act like a cat. He flashed me an insulted look as we approached the registration desk. The doctor was really nice and told me that Mickey had to come back next week when he would get braces. After the inspection Mickey immediately jumped back on my shoulder and we left.

I guess I don't have to tell you what a pain in the neck he was the rest of that week. And he found it necessary to tell me at every opportunity that there were indeed human cat dentists. I did not try to explain to him that this doctor was specialized in cats in general, but just agreed with him.

The day of the appointment had finally arrived and on the way over in the car Mickey kept asking me what I thought was going to happen. I honestly did not know, which I told him. Big mistake! I got all these questions fired at me as to how I could not know, and I should know everything. After 20 minutes I got quite tired of it and asked if he would like to walk the rest of the way, which shut him up for about 2 minutes. After which he realized I would never make true on my threat and started all over with his questions again. I just ignored him the rest of the way.

The doctor's assistant gave Mickey a shot while he was on my shoulder. He warned me to hold on because he would get limp in a few moments. "Mommy, I'm getting sweepyyyyy" was the last thing he said. I waited outside for approximately twenty minutes when I was called into the operating room. Mickey was just regaining consciousness but immediately jumped on my shoulder. He was still a little woozy so I held him tight. What the doctor had done was actually put a little brace on Mickey's teeth. I laughed when I saw it. He had made a lump on his canine tooth and one on his molar tooth and in between there was an elastic band. I was instructed to move the elastic band to the next hole after one week and again the week after and then one more time, before he had to come back.

By the time we got to the car, there was no trace left of the anesthetic and Mickey was his old self again. Well, almost...

"Wommy, thif if annoywing" he said when we got to the car.

"What's that, honey?"

"Thif if vewwy annoywing" he tried again.

"It's okay, darling. Maybe it's beft, I mean, best if you don't talk till you are accustomed to the brace. Perhaps your mouth is a little sore from the procedure." He nodded and just sat quietly on my shoulder, as always, all the way home.

Once we arrived at home he ran into the bedroom and started pawing at the elastic band. I told him to leave it on, that it was good for him and that he would get used to it in no time if he just kept his paws off. But he would not listen and within one hour he had the elastic off on one side of the lump. My husband and I tried to get it back on, but we failed miserably. Mickey is not that big, but we needed two people to restrain him while the third put the elastic back where it belonged. Seeing as there were just two of us, we went to the vet again. That was one expensive visit for two minutes of work. The doctor suggested one of those hoods. We took it with us, but I had already seen by the look on Mickey's face that there was no way he was going to wear that.

I told him that if he left the elastic where it should be that I would not put the hood on him. He promised he wouldn't, but 30 minutes later it was off again. "Oh, this is ridiculous" I cried "I am not taking you back to the vet anymore" I said to Mickey and he smiled thinking he got the best of us. But we had our secret weapon: my brother in law. We called him and he was very willing to help. So two of us held Mickey, while the third re-adjusted the elastic. We also put the hood on immediately. He looked ridiculous but it was his own fault. "That's what happens if you don't keep your promises" I yelled after him as he ran upstairs.

Later that evening, I heard him complaining to the other cats about how cruel we had been. Poor little Mickey, he still had his speech problem caused by the elastic and he had this hood on. All I heard from the other cats was laughter and when I came into the bedroom I saw them all on the bed. Mickey was sitting on the bed announcing our cruelty at top voice and all the others were absolutely floored with laughter. I had never seen such a thing. They were on their bellies or their backs howling with laughter. It was quite funny and I could not help but join in. Poor thing at every word he said, the others would just laugh harder and harder. At a certain point he got so upset I actually thought he was going to explode. So I picked him up and took him downstairs for a moment, keeping my laughter in. That was hard!

"It if not funny, wommy!" Mickey cried.

"No darling it is not, but you should try to rest." I did not want to get into a discussion with him.

"Take thif howwible thing off" he said, feeling very sorry for himself.

"I can't darling, not until you are used to your brace."

"I am ufed to it awweady."

"Are you really?" I asked and looked him deep into his eyes. He turned away from my gaze and knew that he had no choice. "If I were you, I would just keep quiet for a few days, dear. Just till we can take the hood off. Okay?" He nodded, but I could see he was thinking of ways in which he could get the hood off.

After two days Mickey got used to the elastic and we took the hood off. He was no longer the laughing stock in the family, that is, until he opened his mouth. As long as he had that brace he would have a speech problem. We readjusted the elastic band three times just like the doctor instructed.

Finally the day came when the brace was to be removed. Mickey was absolutely happy all the way to the doctor. I heard him humming next to me as he sat in his usual place. I was quite happy also.

Little did I know that it was going to turn out to be a disaster. Of course an anesthetic was needed again, but this time the assistant told me it would take about an hour, instead of telling me to wait, like the first time. So I went for a walk. The facility is huge and I stood watching the horses for almost 40 minutes. After that I returned to the operating room but upon approaching the room I could hear Mickey screaming. The last 100 yards I ran to the room and stood outside panicking. Mickey was crying in absolute terror and there was no one there.

I banged on the door and finally someone opened. They immediately brought me to another room and took Mickey out of his box. Once on my shoulder he immediately shut his mouth. I asked what was wrong with him. The girl sighed and said that because I was not there they had to lock him in a cage until I got back. And Mickey made sure to let them know he did not like that. The girl told me he had managed to break out of three cages until they finally put him in a clothes hamper and they taped it shut. I smiled as an image of this happening passed through my mind. Mickey did not like being locked up, that's for sure. I said to her that I would have been here if they had not told me that the procedure would take an hour. Turned out the one giving the anesthetic was mistaken about what had to be done.

Once in the car I sat with Mickey, apologizing to him as much as I could. "I'm sorry, Mickey, so sorry. It was never my intention to leave you. It was not my fault; they told me it would take an hour. Please forgive me? Please?" and I offered him, his favorite snack. He ignored me for about ten minutes but then he gave in and took his snack, still not speaking to me. "Shall we go home then, dear?" I asked in my most soothing voice. He nodded in approval, but still said nothing and moved to his traveling position. I started the car and was about to drive when he said "I forgive you, Mommy. You're only human" I turned around in delight and lifted him up again. "You can talk!" I cried. He frowned and said "of course I can talk. You know that!" I sighed while I held him in front of me and just let him get the clue which did not take long. His eyes became bright and he shouted "I can talk!" "Yes you can!" and I hugged him.

All the way home he was sitting next to me chattering as he always does. Boy did I miss that voice. In the four weeks he had his brace he hardly said a word, because everybody immediately started to laugh as soon as he started. But he was back and even better. The tooth was now in its place and not hurting him anymore. It had been worth all the trouble.

18.
Dish

A week has gone by since the big fight with Maya. The day after we had a very long talk and I told her she was grounded for a month. This set her off in a rage of fury. She kept telling me that I could not do that to her. How it would upset her social life and, this was my favorite, she would never get a boyfriend. I told her that as long as she lived under my roof, she would live by my rules and that she was way too young for a boyfriend.

She walked away shouting all kind of "nice" wishes to me and tried to go out, but I had told Luke and Bear to make sure that she would not leave. They came in two minutes later with Maya in between them. "In the room with her, Mommy" Luke said to me, so I got up, opened the door to the bedroom and they put her in. I closed the door and heard the shouting and ranting continue inside. "Just let her Mom, she'll get tired soon enough and then I'll have a talk with her" Bear said to me.

Who am I to argue? If he thinks he can get through to her, let him try. So after our little lady had cooled down a bit, Bear went into the room to have a hardy talk with her. I have no idea what he said to her, but two hours later when they came out Maya was completely changed. She promised that she would only leave home to go to school and that she would not go out for the period that I set. I nodded my head in acknowledgement and patted Bear on the head for a job well done. He should have gone into cat psychiatry instead of keeping that bar. There are a lot of loony cats out there and 7 of them are living in my house.

That entire week she slept in our bedroom. Now our cats are not allowed in the bedroom when we go to sleep. However two of them have managed to get an exception on that rule. Luke sometimes sleeps in our room during the day. He says he needs it after a busy night in the club. With all the other cats around he claims he can't relax and needs his solitude. The second who got the exception is, you guessed it, Maya. She sleeps with us in the bedroom at night when she feels like it; when she has no parties to go to, or other social "obligations". She's always very sweet when she's in the bedroom because she realizes very well that it is a privilege that should be cherished. Now what she does when we go to sleep is she crawls on top of my chest and starts talking about her day. During her talks she always gets sleepy and slowly falls asleep. But it also puts me to sleep. She has a really soft and soothing voice and when she speaks it is like a melody. Quite relaxing, really.

And it is better to fall asleep because she makes absolutely no sense in her stories. She assumes that she has told me certain things while I am sure that she has not, but when I ask a question to get a better grasp on the story, she sighs and says that I should pay attention. I really did pay attention in the beginning, but it was impossible to follow. She would begin, then remember something else that happened and talk about that, then go back to the first story but she would not restart where she had left off but somewhere completely different. So now I just listen to that soft voice slowly talking me to sleep.

All I have to do is say the "oh" "ah" and "really" at the right intervals and I'm good. It's a lot more relaxing than reading a book, I'll tell you that.

So this week I got the stories everyday. She would talk about everything that she had discussed with her friends and what they had learned in school that day. Typical teenage cat stuff. And of course all her friends pass the review, Bobbie, Angela, Jennifer, Rodney, Davey, Bobby. I once asked how they kept Bobbie and Bobby apart. Stupid question of course, but I managed to get through to her that the names sound the same. Well in cat language they don't. You could compare it to Bobby (very short) and Bobbieeeeeee (long).

Last night once again she went through the entire cast of cats and with that I don't mean the Broadway show. I was almost asleep when all of a sudden I hear her mentioning Dish. At first I paid no attention to it because I figured she was talking about a time of night. But then she said "... and then Dish said..." and all of a sudden I was wide awake. I opened my eyes and asked her, "Dish? Who is this Dish?" She looked at me, probably surprised at the fact that I was indeed listening to her. She might be gullible but she's definitely not stupid and she knows very well I hardly try to follow her story. "He's a friend" she said casually. "Friend, what kind of friend? Does he go to your school?"

"Oh, heavens no!" she giggled "Dish is too old for school." That got my attention even more. Now I know that age does not make such a difference with cats, but still. I mean if he's not in school that means he must be at least 4 years old. That is like letting your 15 year old daughter have a relationship with a 40 year old man.

Not trying to sound too upset I carefully asked "so what does this Dish do then?"

"He's in sales."

"In sales?"

"Yes, he's a traveling sales cat. He travels all over the country to sell his products." The way she worded that I found a little strange, so I asked her what kind of products this sales cat had."

"All kinds, cat perfume, winter coats, snow boots, delicacies of all sorts, things like that." I was amazed, a cat selling winter coats on Aruba. He must be one smooth talker. But that fact disturbed me a little at the same time. My little girl with such a smooth talker, it did not give me a very good feeling. Maya probably saw my concerns on my face and quickly said "he's very honorable Mommy. He's kind and very intelligent." "I'm sure he is honey" I said trying to sound as normal as possible. So she continued talking about this wonderful Dish. He had done it all, traveling by car, plane and train. I frowned when she said that "ahem, honey"

"Yes Mommy?"

"Where does Dish live?"

"I'm not really sure, but I think it's somewhere near Washington."

"And how do you talk to him?"

"Different ways, sometimes we chat on the computer and sometimes we use skype." I laughed; her friend lived in the US. Far away from us. This was a big relief.

"So tell me Maya, how did you get in contact with him?"

"Well while he is on the road, he sometimes gets lonely so he uses the internet to talk to other cats."

"Aren't there any cat clubs he can go to?"

"Not always. Life on the road can sometimes be very lonely."

I bet it can.

"Don't you find it strange talking to a cat who is so much older then you?"

"He doesn't know how old I really am. He thinks I am three" she giggled.

"Maya! You know you're not supposed to lie!"

"I know Mommy, but it is so cool having an international friend." I could see how that would put her high on the popularity list at school. And what could really happen? It's not like he would ever be able to come here. But there was still one thing I needed to know. "Doesn't he have any owners?"

"Yes, he does, that is why he can do this job so well."

"How so?"

"They travel a lot and he goes with them." And with that it finally all became clear. I was just seeing this cat in my mind traveling all over the United States in cars, trains and by plane. I was wondering how he was doing this. The answer is sometimes so simple. So I went back in my half sleep mode as Maya continued with her story.

That was last night, but just now Maya once again showed that she thinks she is the queen of the house and able to do everything. Remember that I said I had grounded her for a month? Apparently she had decided that one week was more than enough and tonight as I was sitting out on the front porch she walked past me on her way out.

I asked her where in heaven's name she thought she was going and she walked back to me and jumped on the table. I looked at her and decided that she looked absolutely ridiculous.

She had ear clips on her ears, which were so heavy that they pulled her ears down. On closer inspection I saw that they were my earrings. She also had a golden collar which turned out to be one of my most beautiful bracelets. She had golden rings on her paws, a ring on her tail and was completely covered with gold sprinkles.

"Where do you think you are going, young lady?" I demanded to know.

"To Jennifer's party" she announced.

"I don't think so, and most certainly not looking like that!" I pulled off the earrings and took my bracelet off.

"I am going to Jennifer's party" she announced once again.

"You are not! You are grounded for a month, remember?"

"I think a week is more than enough."

"Well you thought wrong."

"That is not fair!" she yelled at me "I behaved for a week, like you told me to and now I can go to Jennifer's party."

"I grounded you for a month as you very well know, that means three more weeks."

"Ah yes, well you see a human month is one week for a cat" she said slyly.

"I'm not stupid Maya. One month is one month. And if you don't stop now I will ground you for another month for taking my jewelry without asking." I saw in her eyes that it was getting through to her that she had blown it, so she tried to get away, but I was too fast for her. I grabbed her and took her to the kitchen. There I removed all the jewelry and cleaned the gold sprinkles out of her fur after which I put her in the room. "No daughter of mine is going out looking like a cheap tramp" I shouted at her as I closed the door. To my surprise there was not a peep from the room all evening.

At dinner time I let her out of the room and she ran into the kitchen. She jumped on the kitchen island and when I got the cans with food she made sure that I noticed her. I ignored her, but she jumped over to the kitchen counter and sat in front of the cans, so I could no longer ignore her. I looked at her curious to find out what she had to say to me.

"You think of me as your daughter?" she asked meekly.

"Yes, I do Maya. Don't you know that?"

"No, I didn't."

"Why do you think I am so upset when you stay out late? Why do you think I worry so much about you?"

"I thought it was because you just wanted to be difficult."

"Oh Maya, no, I am not being difficult. I worry about you and I would not be able to cope with it if something happened to you."

"Why didn't you say so?"

"I did! Why do you think I grounded you?"

"To annoy me!"

I laughed and said "No Maya, I do it because I love you so much" and I grabbed her and held her tight.

"Mommy?"

"Yes dear?"

"Can you let go, I can't breathe" she croaked softly. I did not realize I was squeezing her so tight so I let go immediately.

Meanwhile the boys were all standing behind us looking at the scene. I turned around and saw 12 eyes staring at me. "I love all of you!" I said to them. "You love Maya most!" Jimmy cried. "I don't love Maya most, but she is the only girl in the house, besides me, and that makes her special." I looked at them and saw that they agreed with me. They all liked Maya, even though she is a major pain in the neck sometimes, but somehow she gets away with it. She is just too darn cute and I am the first to admit that I favor her a little. It is a good thing that cats don't really know what jealousy is, and second that they have a short memory for things that don't interest them. At this point they just wanted their food. So I gave it to them.

When she finished eating I asked Maya if she was going to talk to Dish tonight. "I don't know if he gets a change to get online" she answered, a little shy but glad because I was showing interest. "Tell him I said hi" and I smiled at her and patted her cute little head. "I will" she giggled and ran off. I just hope that tomorrow she remembers that she is still grounded.

19.
The dogs

I know that this book is about cats. However the dogs are also a big part of my life and of the cats' lives for that matter. When we moved to Aruba we always said we wanted to get dogs. Two boxers, if possible. And so we did! We got two boxers from the same litter. We got them when they were six weeks old. We named them Angel and Nero. A month before we got the dogs we had found Luke in front of our car gate; a little 6 weeks old kitten whose mother had just been run over by a car. So when the dogs came to our house, Luke was just 10 weeks old, but he is a big cat, so the size difference between him and the puppies wasn't that huge.

They grew up together and as such Luke taught Angel and Nero how to speak. The dogs would see the cats speak to us and as such they also did the same thing. Clubby once explained to me that dogs speak human as cats do, but that their vocabulary is more limited than that of a cat. I got the feeling he was a little biased about that. Our dogs' vocabulary is just as good as that of all the cats, but I think Clubby would say it is because they had great examples in the cats. I can just hear him saying "other dogs are not like that!"

One day, when the dogs were about 10 months old, I was sitting outside catching the last bit of sun of that day. Luke was in the big tree behind our house and the dogs were under it. I could hear Luke saying that they had to come too. So I walked up to the tree and asked what was going on. "Luke, has gone up there and we can't follow" Angel cried. "Well of course not honey, dogs can't climb in trees." They looked at me quizzically, then to each other, then back to me again. Finally Nero spoke "that does not explain why we can't get in the tree." "Yes, it does." "No, it doesn't. You said dogs can't climb in trees. We are cats and we can climb trees." I sighed, how, in heavens' name, was I going to explain this? I squatted down so I was almost at eye level and said "you are dogs." Angel looked up at Luke in the tree and said "Get out of there Luke, you're a dog!" "No darling, Luke is a cat. The two of you are dogs."

"Impossible!" they both shouted in stereo "either Luke is a dog, or we are cats." I asked him how he figured that one.

"Well, cats and dogs don't get along with each other. We get along just fine." If you search very hard there is some logic in that statement. So I explained to them that sometimes cats and dogs get along just fine. I asked them to think how Bear always acted towards them. In the beginning Bear did not appreciate the dogs being in the house. Now he has 'warmed' a little to them, mainly because Angel is such a good cook and he needs him in his nightclub. They thought about it for a minute but concluded that Bear was just overreacting. I had to find another way. So I called Aristotle. "Can you say something in cat for me, Ari?" I asked and he immediately did. I looked at the dogs and said "did you understand any of that?" I should have known better, because, of course they did understand cat because of their close interaction with Luke. "Of course we did Mommy. What a silly question is that." I sighed at my own stupidity and asked them if they could repeat what Ari had just said. They barked at him, which made poor Ari jump up. "That wasn't quite the same, boys." I told Luke, who had come down from the tree, to say the same as Ari did. Of course it was flawless. I looked at the dogs to see if they had heard a difference.

They had not heard any difference. So I tried a different approach. I let one dog say something in cat and let the other listen to the difference. I then switched the dogs and let the other listen. It took me about an hour to convince the dogs that they could not speak cat (even though they could understand it) and that the cats could not speak dog. Aristotle got very tired of the whole experiment and left with a "this is ridiculous" statement.

Luke and the boys stayed behind, a little concerned. "Does this mean we have to start hating each other?" Luke asked quietly. "Oh no, of course not. You guys are good friends and you should stay friends." They were obviously going through some identity crisis. I told them that many dogs and cats were friends. "But how do we know how to act as dogs?" Nero asked slightly panicked. I comforted him by telling that they acted pretty much the way dogs are supposed to act. But if they wanted I could see if there was a school they could go to and learn dog stuff. I called Goofy to see what he knew in this area. Being head master of a kitten school surely he must have some contacts. Indeed he did. Goofy made all the arrangements and even took the dogs to school the first day. I asked him if that would not make the dogs the laughing stock of school. After all, there aren't that many cats that bring dogs to school. But he assured me that the other dogs would never see him. He's very smart, my Goofy, he would hide behind a bush and see to it that the dogs entered the school and in the afternoon he would wait for them behind that same bush and take them home again.

So my dogs were not the laughing stock of the entire school. They were happy to go to school. Socializing with other dogs was good for them. Nero loved it on the track team and Angel felt really at home in the wrestling team. I never had any dogs before so I didn't know what they teach them there. I know in cat school they learn reading, writing, mathematic, some geography and other things we humans learn in school. But also physical exercise and a class I really don't appreciate that much: how to manipulate your human. Kitten school is mostly about playing and physical exercise and in the higher education they can choose to learn about a certain trade like becoming a nurse, cat doctor, teacher, private investigator, sales cat etc.

With dogs I found out that it was more about physical exercise and more about how to intimidate others; so the biting, jumping, barking, snarling, things like that. Angel and Nero always told me everything they had learned in school that day and they had classes such as "how to defend your human", which is one I actually appreciated. That it was lost on my dogs is beside the fact. Ever since their first lesson in that class they have been bugging me to get a guard dog. I once asked them for whom the guard dog was intended. You don't want to know the answer.

And of course it turned out dogs also have a class called: how to manipulate your human. They teach the dogs sad faces, happy faces, disgruntled faces etc. My dogs got an A+ for the sad faces, but I did not find that a great accomplishment at all; they're boxers and that says it all.

While the cats can go to school for at least 6 years, for dogs it's only 2 years. I think I now understand what Clubby meant when he said that dogs were more practical than theoretical. Okay, he said it differently; I'm just rephrasing it into nicer words. It's not that dogs can't learn as much and as well as cats, it's just that they have no interest in it. It goes so far that in some classes they actually have cat teachers, because they can't get a dog teacher. Now you might think, dogs learning from cats? I know I was as surprised as you are when I found out, but the act they put up when humans are around is totally different than when they are "amongst" each other. Of course there are always those cats and those dogs who don't know about the schools and the interaction that normally goes on between them (and all animals for that matter) and those are the ones that really hurt each other. I suppose it's the way the world is.

The dogs don't have as many adventures as the cats do, simply because they are home more often. They also don't care as much about things as the cats do. Clubby would say they are simple. But they do care about certain things. They care about playing, going to the beach as often as possible, their food and their daily hug. They also make it clear they want to be near us as much as possible. Sometimes when I leave the house they almost cry. It gets a little better when I promise them I won't be long. Then they try their sad face on me and I tell them they really deserved that A+. That makes them smile immediately.

Today, Maya is the only one who does not get along with the dogs. She calls them dragons. Maybe it is best that she's a little afraid of them. Makes her more cautious for other dogs as well, which is a good thing for when she's leaves home.

I count my blessings for having these two wonderful dogs and I would not know what to do without them.

20.
Fire!

To say that today was an eventful day, is an understatement. Let me begin at the beginning of this story which was a few days ago.

In the spare moments I have during the day, I like to visit bulletin boards on the internet. There is one in particular that I visit a lot, to help people who are planning their trip to Aruba. I have met some great people that way and some of them are now very close friends. Well a few days ago there was this request from a lady if anyone was willing to take her dog to Canada for her.

Now you may ask how this came to be. Let me tell you. This lady was on Aruba a few weeks ago and she found a street dog that was rather sick. She was kind enough to bring the animal to the vet and she was given three choices. First choice was to release the dog back to the street and let her fend for herself. With the dog being very sick, she would probably not last very long. The second choice was to put the dog to sleep and the third choice was to operate on the cancer she had and try to make her better after which she could join the nice lady back in her homeland Canada. Needless to say that she opted for the third choice. That was a few weeks ago and just recently the dog was given a clean bill of health and she was ready to travel to her new home. So this lady, Kathleen, posted a message on the bulletin board asking if someone traveling to Canada could take the dog with them as baggage.

Now since I live here I could not ever take the dog anywhere. Wanting to help I offered my house so that the dog would not have to stay in the animal shelter until that time. I figured she could play with my two boys and was told that she got along very well with cats.

Yesterday I got a call asking if I could pick her up today in the afternoon. So that's what I did. I took Angel and Nero with me to see how they would react to her. If they would immediately start to fight the whole deal was off naturally. Before we left for the animal shelter I explained to the boys what was going to happen and asked them to show their very best behavior. "Don't we always" was their offended answer to which I did not respond, because the answer would be "no" anyway.

On the way over I got all these questions fired at me. "What's her name?"

"It's Kunuku Princess of Aruba."

"How fast can she run?"

"Excuse me?"

"How fast can she run?" Nero, repeated his question. Of course being on a track team he's always looking for competitors.

"I have absolutely no idea" I answered in all honesty.

"Can she wrestle?" This time it was Angel. Guess what he does in his spare time...

"I doubt it, honey."

"Well if she can't run fast and she can't wrestle, why is she coming to live with us?"

"I already explained that to you before we left home."

"I wasn't listening. Can you repeat the story?" Nero asked.

"No, now shut up and sit still!"

"Humans!" was the last thing I heard until we got to the vet's office.

The excitement started up again as we got out of the car. The meeting was quite uneventful. They sniffed at each other and the boys lost their interest in about two seconds. When I got a second alone with them I asked them what was going on and it turned out they could not understand her. "What do you mean you can't understand her? I whispered at them "don't you speak dog?" "Yes, we do" they whispered at me "but she speaks a different kind of dog." "What do you mean a different kind of dog?" I demanded to know. "Just what I said, but here she comes again" Nero said and sat up straight as if nothing was going on.

So I took her in the car and we drove home. Louise from the Animal Rights organization, in charge of Kunuku's traveling plans, went along to see if she would get along with the cats. When we got home the cats were just having their 5 o'clock snack. What happened next no one would have been able to foresee.

Bear saw Kunuku first and being a big coward of all that is strange he fled and then it happened. Seeing a cat run away is, of course, an incentive for any dog and that is exactly what Kunuku wanted to do. She was on her leash, but it was a bit long as she jumped forward up against the kitchen island. The other cats also saw her. Maya went into a complete panic and tried to get away through the kitchen window, but in her panic landed on top of the stove. Dinner was being prepared for that evening and as such I had a skillet full of boiling hot oil on the stove. Still in a panic Maya again tried to get away and once again jumped on the stove but this time she managed to get out of the door. Louise in the meantime had managed to get Kunuku out of the kitchen. But the damage was done. I ran outside after Maya, hoping that I could find her, but I didn't.

While I was out looking for Maya, my husband was inside, talking to Louise and discussing Kunuku. When I came back in we discussed what was to be done and decided that Kunuku would stay with us today and we would see how things would go. It is obvious that the Princess is a friendly dog, but evidently feels that cats are fun to run after. We had a quick bite and then my husband took it upon himself to teach Kunuku some manners and most importantly to teach her that cats are not animals you ought to run after.

During the training Mozes was constantly walking behind my husband and Kunuku (at a safe distance). Mozes is a bit of a sensationalist. He's never in the fight or the event, but he's always on the front row seat looking at it all. Sometimes when I call him for dinner late in the evening he doesn't show up. But I always keep on calling until he appears. Finally when I go to the front gate to see if he is somewhere on the street he suddenly appears next to me. Looking outside as if to say "so who are we looking for now?" I just look at him and he then grins and runs inside knowing very well I was looking for him. But I digress (again...)

Every ten minutes I called out to see if Maya was ready to come in. But the entire evening there was no sign of her. I did get Luke's company for a better part of the evening. He was sitting next to me, while Kunuku, Angel and Nero were laying on the floor at my feet. "Why does she do that?" Luke finally asked after staring at Kunuku for almost 20 minutes. What could I say? "I have no idea, Luke. Maybe she had previous owners who taught her to chase cats."

"But that's not nice" he said indignantly.

"I agree, but you can't blame her for things that bad owners taught her."

"I guess not, but still, it's not nice."

"I agree with you Luke, but what can we do about it?"

"Tell her to stop it!"

"How? She doesn't speak the same dog as Angel and Nero, so that's not an option."

"What do you mean?" Luke cried and turned to the dogs "talk to her and tell her not to chase us!"

"We tried, Luke" Angel responded "but she doesn't understand us"

"Oh, what good are you" and he jumped off the table and walked out of the room. Angel and Nero scurried after him apologizing. I shook my head and once again went searching for Maya.

It was over three hours since she had run off and I was worried to death. This time I wasn't going to stop looking until I had found her. After I had spent about twenty minutes walking around the yard and beyond, I came back in and was almost in tears because I couldn't find my little darling. I was about to give up when I heard a tiny voice behind me say "Mommy..." I looked around and saw my Mayalina. I grabbed her and immediately took her into our bedroom. "Mommy, it hurts" she cried very softly. "I know it does, honey. Don't worry, Mommy is going to make you all better." "Promise?" she said quietly. "I promise." I said, more confident than I was. Every sole under her little paws was burned. Some of it so bad that there was no callus left and the flesh was visible. Others had big blisters or pieces of skin falling off them. Her left paw was so bad that a piece of her flesh was burned away around one of her nails. Higher up her legs she had some really nasty burns that just looked horrible. She was completely covered in oil. The only positive thing I could see was that it was mostly her front paws and her face and body were not burned. The poor thing could not put any weight on her front paws and sat on her back legs like a rabbit.

Luckily we had some anti-biotic ointment in house and I dressed her paws carefully. She was so tired and still a little in shock so she did not object to me putting the dressings on her paw. I made a nice little bed for her and put her to sleep under a little blanket. It was clear that the bandages did help reduce the pain a little and after a while she fell asleep.

I left her alone and turned my attention to Kunuku. It was important that she learned not to chase the cats, so she was learning the most important word for all dogs: NO.

She's an intelligent dog. She's already starting to listen. But perhaps that's because we give her little nibbles when she does something right.

One other thing I noticed is that she is very jealous. Angel came up to me while I was teaching her to sit and she ran up to him and growled at him. It was in a protective kind of way.

Angel gave her a rather contemptuous look, but one "aha" from me, reminded him of his promise to behave. He walked away to complain to his brother about our houseguest. I'm sure he found a willing ear in Nero. Too bad the boys can't talk to her. They could explain everything to her and we would not have to go through so much trouble.

Tonight we will put her in our second bathroom. I am not letting her roam free in the yard or the living room. We can't have her going after any of the cats during the night. Tomorrow I will have a talk with all of them. If they just don't run away from her, she won't go after them. It's obvious that, this is the fun behind it all. I don't think she wants to hurt them, but just run after them. When I closed up for the night, I got sounds of protest from my two boys. They found it really unfair that Kunuku was allowed to sleep inside while they had to sleep outside.

They always sleep outside and never have any problem with it and that is what I told them. "But then there wasn't another dog who was allowed to sleep inside!" They cried in stereo at me. I asked them if they wanted to sleep in the bathroom and they looked at each other, then turned to me and unanimously shook their heads. It was not what they wanted. "Then stop whining and go to bed" I told them and they did without further protest.

Before turning in for the night I tried to get Maya to eat a little which she did. This was a good sign. However she was very tired and immediately went back to sleep. The dressing was still on. Apparently she did not try to take it off.

I am also going to sleep now. What a day! And what will tomorrow bring?

21.
What a difference a few days make

The last two days I haven't had much sleep. Maya is sleeping in our room and every two hours she wakes up and calls me. So I bring her something to drink, or a little bit to eat or I just hold her. Yesterday we took off the dressings on her paws. She immediately started to lick her paws and she removed some loose skin here and there. It's amazing how cats just know how to do certain things. She will not touch the blisters that are not completely "done" yet and will lick around them. She has hardly said a word only the utmost necessary. She looks a little scruffy so I offered to clean her a little with a soft cloth. She said she didn't want it. Poor thing, she's really feeling sorry for herself and I don't blame her. The new bandages seem to help her feel a little more comfortable. Of course I use plenty of ointment on her blisters. I don't want her paws to get infected.

As for Kunuku yesterday we tried to see if she had learned anything from the lessons all day but unfortunately, as soon as Aristotle took off, so did she. He is fast for a 14 year old cat! He climbed into a tree and sat there hissing at Kunuku. So we locked her in the bathroom for 15 minutes or so. She absolutely hates being alone. Well maybe this way it will get through to her that chasing cats is a big no no in our house.

Luke and Mozes follow us and Kunuku everywhere we go. Angel and Nero are complaining that we don't give them enough attention. Bear is saying how it messes up his entire schedule and Goofy said he can't place her in any school. And they all do it at the same time. They are driving me absolutely nuts! I tried to convince Goofy that he does not have to find her any school, because she won't be with us that long. But he just keeps nagging about it. I wonder if he gets a commission for referring dogs to the dog school.

Today things weren't much better. Jimmy and Aristotle still take off when they see Kunuku. She got to know Luke's sharp claws and ever since that moment she has the greatest respect for him. But Luke is a rat! He is following Kunuku everywhere she goes and when she shows interest in himr he smacks her. I called him and told him that he shouldn't be so annoying. "I think I am in my right here" Luke announced to me.

"Luke, she is a house guest and you should treat her accordingly."

"This is how I treat house guests."

"You hit your guests?"

"I do, if they come too close."

"But she doesn't come close to you, you go to her!"

"What's your point? She gets too close doesn't she?"

I sighed, after two nights of hardly sleeping this was not the type of conversation I wanted to have.

"Just stay away from her okay?"

"Typical human, when you can't win with arguments you just forbid us to do something, hoping that it will resolve the situation! Well, we'll see about that!" Luke cried rebelliously.

"Luke! I am warning you. Mommy is not in the mood for your antics." He gave me one last defiant look and walked into the house.

Today we have been doing some more training with Kunuku. We are keeping her on a leash now. She listens very well when we do that, but once she is loose, she'll go after any cat that will run. I've been trying to convince Aristotle that if he does not run, she will not come after him. "Just look at Goofy" I told him, but he's just too afraid and runs away. I haven't seen Jimmy for the last two days. He comes in at night to eat and after that he's gone again. I asked Bear where he was going "How should I know? My entire schedule is disrupted!" was his answer. Luckily Mo came to my rescue and told me he was hiding way in the back of the yard. "Thank you Mo, glad to see that at least one of my cats is still sane." He smiled a big smile and I honestly believe he was glowing with pride. "All thanks to Yoga!" he said and walked away to take a nap. Or some more yoga exercises? I really can't tell the difference.

I am spending a lot of time with this house guest. It is obvious that she is a kind dog and she really wants to play. This morning she started jumping around in front of Luke in a very playful way. Luke just ignored her and when she didn't go away he hissed at her. That cooled her off somewhat. We want her to socialize with the dogs, the cats and with humans.

What surprised us is that she is not in the least interested in toys. We tried a squeaky toy, but Angel and Nero ran off with it. Another thing that is also very interesting. Whenever I call one of my boys, and start to pet them, she wriggles herself in between me and Angel or Nero and when they don't immediately leave she growls at them. Of course that is a big no, no, but a stern "Kunuku!", puts her in her place. I don't know why she does that. Whether it's jealousy or if she feels she has to protect me from those big mean dogs. When she does that, the boys just look at her like "are you kidding me?" and turn around. I suspect they laugh at her behind her back.

It's a good thing that Angel and Nero are so gentle. Any other dog would probably have started a big fight with her to put her in her place. But they just go out and play with each other like always.

She is also completely fixated on food. The first two days she would gobble down her food and then head for the bowls of Angel and Nero. And those big dufusses just let her. So we have to stay and wait until everybody has emptied their bowl and then we can let Madam go. Too bad for her there is a bottom on every bowl. She does appreciate the bologna snack before going to bed. It's a nighttime snack we always give the dogs before they go to bed. Hope we are not teaching her bad manners. But then again, one slice of bologna before going to bed, how bad can that be?

This evening I removed Maya her dressings from last night. Her paws look good, as far as they can. No infection, but they are starting to itch. "Can you leave the bandages off, Mommy?" she asked me when I wanted to put new ones on. "You think that is wise, dear?"

"The bandages itch so much. Please?"

"Well, we can try and see how it looks tomorrow."

"Thank you, Mommy. Can I have something to eat now?" I walked out and got her something delicious. But I have to hold it up for her. She can't put any weight on her front paws and sits upright like a rabbit. She is starting to clean herself a little but gets tired soon. This is going to take a long time and she does not want me to help.

When she finished eating I sat with her in my arms for while. "Mommy?" "Yes Maya?"

"When is that fire breathing dragon going to leave?"

"Soon Maya, very soon."

"I'm afraid of it."

"I know you are honey. But don't worry; I am not letting her near you anyway." I was going to try to explain to her that the burns were caused by the stove. For her the dog and the fire were linked and I was never going to be able to explain otherwise to her.

We have to find some way to get Maya outside every now and then. And we have to find a way to let Kunuku in the living room at night. Locking her up in the bathroom is not a good solution. But what can we do? She's not to be trusted with the cats when we are not around. Maybe tonight when I am supposed to sleep the inspiration will hit me. I sure hope Maya will sleep through the night tonight. I don't know if I can take another sleepless night.

22.
Things are starting to get better

Well 2 more sleepless nights. Maya was constantly asking for attention. "Mommy, scratch my belly. Mommy, give me some food. Mommy, I'm thirsty!" Sometimes I envy my husband who just sleeps through it all. However I did come up with a solution for the "locking in the bathroom" problem. During the day we keep Kunuku on a long leash. It's hot anyway so she doesn't feel a whole lot like running after the cats. She wants to stay in the shade anyway. Absolutely hates the sun! I was thinking that perhaps when we leave (weekend is over and we have to go to work again) we could tie her in the hallway on a shorter leash. The hallway has no furniture and so she will be able to move freely but not run the chance of wrapping herself around some piece of furniture. That is a very real possibility if we tie her in the living room on her long leash.

I had to leave for a short while yesterday, so I tried it. It worked like a charm. The cats were sleeping in the kitchen and living room when I came home and Kunuku was still sound asleep in the hallway. We are definitely going to do this from now on. I am sure she will be much happier sleeping in front of our bedroom door instead of the bathroom. I just wish there was a way I could talk to her and make her understand not to chase the cats. Then she would be able to roam freely in the house and yard. She is also still on her food fixation. When we are home we tie her on her long leash somewhere in the living room. She can then reach the living room and the kitchen. She sleeps most of the day anyway, and I wonder if she even knows she is tied up. She must know, she's reminded of it every time she tries to chase Aristotle. He now knows she can't reach him. Finally!

Anyway I was telling you about her food fixation. Because she can get into the kitchen she reaches with her paws to the cat dishes on the kitchen island and throws them on the floor. One angry look from me does the trick and she scurries away. Like I said, she is very smart, but just hopes she can get away with certain things. In that way animals are just like children.

That is how she spent her day yesterday: just lying around the house sleeping most of the time and getting used to a normal family life. She is learning that the cats are also part of the household. Luke still feels it is fair to smack Kunuku every chance he gets. And to make an even bigger impression he curves his back and hisses in his lowest and meanest voice. I would be afraid if I were Kunuku and I do think she believes Luke is an evil red monster.

I don't know if Kunuku ever had an owner, but it is obvious that even though she is sweet, she is absolutely clueless to who is the boss. She sees no reason why she should listen to us. It almost seems as if she is willing to please us in return for some bologna. Her new owner is going to be in for quite a challenge. I hope she's up to it.

Maya is still feeling very sorry for herself. Her right paw is obviously worse than her left one. She does not want the bandages on anymore. She says it makes her paws irritated. I am going to try and find some breathable bandages. Cats sweat through their paws, so I can imagine if we pack her paws too tight that it will get hot, sweaty and irritable. While she was sleeping yesterday morning I noticed that higher up her paw (even higher than where I had noticed it before) she also has a big blister. I did not see it at first because there was still some fur in front of it, but that is starting to come loose now. Have to find a way to dress that as well.

Yesterday afternoon when I came in to check on her, our little princess announced that she was going out. I asked her if she thought that would be the best thing to do. She said it was "I need to walk a little to keep up my strength". I told her to wait and I put Kunuku in the kitchen so that Maya would not see her after which I let her out of the room. I followed her as she slowly walked to the front door. Her paws were not dressed so it was her painful little paws on the tiles. She was very determined and walked straight from the front porch onto the paved yard. The stones were hot, from the sun blazing on it all day and it even hurt on my feet, so I was really worried what she would do.

The moment she set foot on a hot spot she softly meowed, but continued walking. "Maya, if it hurts you should not continue" I told her quietly. "Shut up Mommy!" she yelled at me and continued walking while growling at every step. I don't think she meant to yell, but she was just so frustrated. Being cooped up in a room all day and then you go out and your paws hurt. I could imagine how she felt. I let her walk around a little more but stayed real close. That way if something went wrong I would be able to grab her immediately. After ten minutes

I grabbed her and carried her inside. She was obviously tired although she denied it completely "let me go, let me go!" "You're tired, Maya, and your feet hurt. Let's go inside and you can walk again tonight when the floor is not so hot." That promise made her quiet down and she let me take her back to the bedroom.

I kept my promise. In the evening I took her out to the back yard. However this time I put a halter on her with a leash (still had those from when we walked Clubbie) and followed her. Why the leash you ask? I didn't want her to be startled by something and run off to somewhere where I couldn't find her or get to her. She would not be able to defend herself with those paws yet. So she stays close to me, or rather I stay close to her. After ten minutes of walking around really slow she curled up and fell asleep. I just grabbed my laptop, sat by her and worked while she slept.

Today when I walked Kunuku I noticed how she absolutely hates being in the sun. She moves from tree to tree and really does not want to go out for a walk during the day. Good thing she's moving to Canada. In Canada the sun is not as bright and as hot as here in the tropics, especially in the winter. I wonder how she will react to snow.

This evening we all sat outside for a while and Angel and Nero started playing with their rope. They like the pulling game especially when someone joins in the game. We tried to get Kunuku in on the fun and at a certain point she actually did! It was nice to see her play for the first time. However at a certain point she got the rope all to herself and when Nero tried to grab it, she growled at him. Nero looked at me all upset and said "Mommy, she's not playing nice! Tell her to play nice." I told him that he knew very well that I could not talk to her, and he couldn't either. He did not like the fact I reminded him of that. They just sat there looking really sorry for themselves, so after a few minutes I said "just go get your rope, you are stronger than she is" They did just that but they are so kind and nice that as she walked away with the rope they grabbed it at the far edge, as far away from her as possible and pulled it back. It was fun to see. But she is jealous! She has never learned to share.

All the time we still had her on her leash and just when we thought she wouldn't do it anymore, she spotted Bear and went after him. Just for a second I did not have the leash in my hand and she grabbed her opportunity. We finally got hold of her again, shook her, and locked her in the bathroom. That's her cooling off place. She hates it and we hope she associates the bad place with bad behavior. It is strange though, Luke, Mozes and Goofy are no fun to her. They don't run away or they smack her, so she leaves them alone. But the others are not safe.

Tonight's incident got us believing that she was not always a street dog, but that she was taught to go after cats. They are truly an obsession for her. She has two obsessions in her life: Cats and food.

Anyway another day passed without too many incidents. And as I write this last entry in my diary, Maya is sleeping in my arms on the table. She is obviously feeling better and fed up with being in our bedroom. I dressed her paws again with some special bandages I bought. I also bought special burn medication ointment and when she walked outside she did not meow at every step. I guess it is helping ease the pain. However, she is trying to pull them off every time.

She is going to be fine, but she will be glad when that fire breathing dragon has left the house. I tried to convince her that Kunuku is not a fire breathing dragon, but she won't hear of it. I guess the story can only get more fantastic with every day, which I am sure it will. In a year from now, she will probably be telling this to other cats, in such a way, that you cannot imagine how she ever survived. I can just hear it now "and with my last breath I dragged myself back to the house..." Cats! They certainly have a flair for the dramatic and mine are absolute champions at it.

23.
Gremlin

Yesterday morning I got a call from the Animal Right Foundation informing me they found someone willing to take Kunuku to her new home. Of course I made the big mistake of telling everyone and I don't think I am ever going to hear the end of it.

Things did not go exactly as planned and in the evening I received a call that Kunuku was not going anywhere. When I told the dogs she was leaving they told me that it was cruel to take away their guard dog. I told them she was never their guard dog, but only a guest. They did not agree with me on that and we argued about it all day. I finally ended the discussion by reminding them that they ignored her the entire day anyway, so they wouldn't even know if she was here or not. That shut them up.

There was one moment where I actually believed that Angel would be happy if she left. Kunuku was standing in front of Angel waiting for her dinner and she was happily whooshing her tail from one side to the other. Angel was sitting close behind her and she was hitting him in the face with her tail. All I heard while I was preparing their food was "ooh, ah, ooh, ah". Finally I turned to him "Angel just move away if it hurts so much."

"It doesn't hurt Mommy. It is just a little annoying."

"So is your complaining. Just move away so she doesn't hit you in the face." Do I really have to tell you that he didn't and just kept at it until dinner was served?

There was of course also the bone incident. But this time the boys decided it was enough. Thinking this morning she was going home I bought her a rawhide bone. That way she would have something to chew on in the airplane. Of course Angel and Nero were absolutely insulted by the fact they did not get a bone so they decided to steal hers. In their attempt to do so Kunuku defended her bone by growling at the both of them. But this time she had gone too far and Nero growled back. She immediately backed off and Nero was ready to run with her bone, but I stopped him. I told him that this bone was not his and he should leave it alone. Very reluctantly he moved away from the bone and Kunuku immediately grabbed it back. It is completely gone now; so much for keeping something for the trip.

Anyway, after hearing the news that Kunuku was not leaving I had to tell everyone. It goes without saying that all the cats were angry with me. All my attempts at explaining that it was not my fault fell on deaf ears and they all decided that they would all ignore me "until she's gone!" Bear yelled at me before leaving for the club. Only Maya said she still loved me even though I did not keep my promise. I thought it was sweet of her to say that. It won't be so bad. They'll forget soon enough. I suspected that around dinnertime I would be forgiven and I was right.

I did take Maya to the doctor today. I noticed that her right paw was bleeding and I wanted to be sure that everything was okay. The doctor told me not to dress the paw anymore and he gave me some antibiotic pills for her to take. These pills are just a precaution because one of the burns was a little irritated. He said we did a very good job with her, which I was glad to hear. On the way home she fell asleep on my lap. Poor thing, normally she would be ready to go play but now she's so tired. Just like humans. If you are sick you are tired faster and you need your sleep.

Just as I came home from the doctor's office Yessie came to visit. She wanted to see Kunuku one last time before she left for Canada. Yessie works in the vet's office where they operated on Kunuku. She took care of Kunuku during all that time. Now Yessie truly has a heart of gold. She takes care of all kinds of animals that are brought in sick or that she finds. And I mean all kinds of animals: dogs, cats, pigs, bird, ducks, donkeys and anything else you can think of. She sees animals in the most deplorable condition. Animals that have been abused, hurt, in an accident etc. I admire her greatly because I doubt if I would be able to deal with such misery.

It was a happy reunion between the two of them. When she finished greeting Kunuku she turned to me and showed me a box that she had taken with her. In the box there was a little kitten of approximately three weeks old. Yessie told me he was abandoned by his mother at one of the hotels. Now I have always wanted to bottle feed a cat and raise it from baby. She asked me if I wanted to take care of the little thing. Would I ever? Of course I would! He is just so adorable.

For now we have named him Gremlin, because he looks a little like one. I'm sure we will think of a better name soon. After Yessie left I introduced the little one to the dogs and the cats that were around. Kunuku and Nero just went wild thinking I had brought them a toy. Angel is absolutely crazy about the little one and wants to lick him all the time. Aristotle reacted the same way he always does when a kitten is introduced in our house; he ignored him.

Bear asked me if he could use him in an act in his club and when I said no, he walked away heavily insulted. Goofy looked him over, sniffed him here and there, nodded approvingly and announced that I most certainly would have to place him on the waiting list for kitten school. He pulled out a piece of paper and asked me what the name of his new pupil was. I shook my head and proceeded to introduce him to the rest of the crowd. Mozes said he was not interested in another kitten, Jimmy screamed and ran and Luke did nothing but hiss at him. I told him not to overreact so much, but he looked at me and said "first you bring in that dragon who almost tried to kill me and now you bring in this monster and you are telling me not to overreact?"

"He is not a monster; he's a little kitten, Luke!"

"Uhuh, yeah right! Well I don't believe you. You also said that dragon would leave! And did he? Huh? Did he?" I saw he was getting rather hysterical so I left. I don't know why Luke always reacts so dramatically. Could it have to do something with the color of his fur? I mean are red cats more emotional than others? Luke is my first red cat ever, so I have no other reds to compare him to.

I cannot say that the introduction of the Gremlin to Maya went any better "Mini dragon, mini dragon!" she screamed when I showed him to her. I sighed and left. I had a little kitten to feed and was not about to start an argument with my other cats at this point. That is what I did the rest of the day. Feed kitten and Angel was always there to help me with the cleaning. He is such a darling. He is obviously seeing me as his mother because he loves to crawl up in my arms and sleep after the feeding. He'll sleep in the bedroom for now. Maya will just have to get used to the fact.

I am keeping him away from Nero and Kunuku. They are just not careful with such a little baby. They think it's a toy and if they are not careful they will crush him. I mean he is still so little that whenever he shakes his little head, he topples over. So cute!

This is my first "baby" cat. I hope I do well.

24.
Friday the 13th

Okay, so Luke found it necessary to fight with the neighbors' cat last night. He obviously hurt his paw because he's limping and somehow managed to blame it on the new kitten, my hero. Then I see Mo at 8 AM he's fine, I see him again at 9 and he's holding an ice pack to his eye. Have no idea what went wrong there and I am not getting any answer either because he won't talk to me.

Kunuku and Nero get in "play" mode when they see the Gremlin. You know how that is, they stretch out their front paws, lower their head, arse up in the air, tail wagging and then they start jumping around from side to side. Too bad Kunuku jumps on Nero and that is not appreciated so they get into an argument, like, "watch where you're going bitch", "Oh jerk, you watch it". As I stood there watching them I realized that for once the "B" word was used correctly.

Goofy is following me all over the house, telling me I should put the new kitten on the waiting list for kitten school as soon as possible, otherwise he can't guarantee a place when he's six weeks old. I told him I'm not sure the kitten is staying here and if that is the case he would have to go to another school. He stopped for a minute and laughed at me.

"What?" I said. "Oh Mommy, please, you really think that after you have raised this little kitten you are going to let it live with other people? Really Mommy, you insult me! You know as well as I do that this kitten is going nowhere. You better just sign him up now and get it over with." I told him to leave me alone. I was in no way going to admit that he was right.

Angel found it his task to become the substitute mother for the little one. Maya is feeling sorry for herself because she has to take the pills the doctor gave me and starts whining the moment I enter the room. And that is just the first hour that I was awake of Friday the 13th. I had a splitting headache and took an aspirin and went to bed. At that moment I was thinking of not coming out of bed for the rest of the day, but I did.

The aspirin took care of the headache. Of course as soon as I showed my head outside the bedroom Goofy was there again with his list. I told him that if he did not leave me alone he would find his list you know where. He left complaining to his brother how rude Mommy was.

I have noticed that Kunuku is getting more and more relaxed. At first she was very hyper and nervous. She is getting calmer, obviously more at ease. She doesn't jump up at me as much as she did at first. I think she will be a great pet, once she gets used to the cats. I hope her new owner doesn't have cats and if she does, I hope they don't run away like mine did in the beginning. Except for Jimmy they are now all used to Kunuku. And of course Maya is still convinced she's a fire breathing dragon. But she has to stay in our bedroom until her paws are significantly better anyway, so she isn't leaving the room any time soon. And when she does, I hope that Kunuku is in her new home.

There was one thing I keep forgetting to tell you about Kunuku. In our yard we have these things that we call "pica". A pica is a small seed from an indigenous plant of Aruba and the seed has three very sharp thorns. You could compare their shape to those crow feet they use to throw under a driving car in the movies. So you can imagine what happens when you step in them. Let me tell you, it hurts. Now whenever Angel or Nero steps in one of them, they hobble on three paws to me and I take it out for them. I have even seen Nero run on two paws (both right or both left) instead of three or four. Absolutely amazing, that dog is so athletic. But I digress: sometimes the pica has already fallen out by the time they get to us, but we still have to rub their paw so they know it's out. Sometimes they are not so bright. And then the whining! "Mommy, Mommy it hurts!!" And when I pull it out they go "ouch, ouch, ouch!" They are big babies. I raised two baby boxers.

Anyway what I noticed with Kunuku is that whenever she gets one of those pica's in her paw she pulls them out herself with her front teeth. She goes about it very efficiently. The other day, she couldn't get it out so I lifted her paw pulled it out, rubbed her soles like I do with the boys, but she didn't believe me. She had to go see for herself that the pica was actually out. It has happened a few times since and every time she looks and sees if indeed it is gone. Little non-believer!

At this moment the little Gremlin is sleeping on the table in front of me. I just fed him. Boy, those baby nails are sharp.

I did have a big laugh with him earlier today. I spilled some of his milk on the kitchen counter and he found it. But he obviously does not know how to lick (yet) and was trying to suck it up. I laughed so hard at the little slurping sounds, I startled the little thing. Whenever I give him his bottle he goes absolutely wild. I finally figured out the best way to do it and not get those little nails in every finger (and worse under my nails!) of my hand. He's like a little cactus that jumps at you and sometimes holds on. You should see my hands! I am not complaining I am loving every minute of it. This is just what the doctor ordered.

And to end this day, I have some good news. This afternoon I received the good news that a nice couple have presented themselves and are willing to take Kunuku with them tomorrow. Now I made the mistake of telling everyone that she was leaving before so this time I am going to keep my mouth shut. They will find out soon enough when I put her in the car and return without her...

25.
Going home

This morning I got up early for a Saturday morning. I walked Kunuku and I fed her. Normally the dogs don't get breakfast but since she was traveling today I gave her some food. She won't be getting any food for a while and she can't fly with a full stomach. She won't be getting anything in the plane either. I hope this food will keep her happy until she arrives at her new home. After I hooked her up I fed the Gremlin and I put the Gremlin on the litter box and he did use it! Amazing for a kitten of a little over three weeks old. He is one smart kitten. I fed Maya and gave her the medication. Of course she heavily resisted. Then I fed the other cats who were insulted by the fact they were last on the list.

I left for the airport around 1 PM and of course took Kunuku with me. The boys were not at all happy that I left without them. They were sure that she was going to the beach and I was leaving them at home. So I explained to them that she was going to the airport to fly to her new mommy. They turned their backs on me and as I backed out of the yard, I heard Angel say "traitor!". I stopped and told him that I was really going to bring Kunuku to the airport and that I was coming back without her. "Trust me, will ya" I said to him. He looked at me and I could see that he wanted to believe me, but going to the beach is something almost sacred to them and if I am leaving in the car I am going to the beach. Always!

As I arrived at the airport Kunuku jumped out of the car as soon as I parked the car and opened the door to get out. I am so used to my boys waiting till I open the door and say that it's okay for them to go out, that I never gave it a second thought that Kunuku of course does not know that. She ran off and I ran after her, chasing her down the parking lot. Luckily she had that long rope attached to her collar and I was able to catch her after ten minutes of running around. Okay, that did not really happen but I did see it happening in my mind. I could just see myself running after her and the dog getting away at the last moment. Things like that always happen to me. Thank goodness for that long leash. I stepped on it quickly and grabbed her. A close call, a very close call.

We both walked up to the departure hall. She is just such a happy dog. I asked myself if she knew in any way that she was going to her new owner. Start a new life in a foreign country? I doubt it, and even I was able to talk to her I doubt if I could explain it all to her. I still remember the trouble I had explaining the move from Holland to Aruba to the cats. In the departure hall we waited together for about three minutes when two people came up to me and asked me if that was Kunuku. Indeed it was. Jeff and Carole had found me. Lovely people! Jeff took his place in the check-in line while Carole and I waited for Louise, who had the cage and the papers. She arrived shortly after. Kunuku was highly interested in the cage so I put her in it. It was a good way for her to get used to it and not be afraid. They had to weigh the cage with Kunuku in it anyway. Louise told me she gained weight during the week she was with us. I guess we did a good job. Before Jeff and Carole went through the gates with Kunuku we walked her a little. After all she will have no way to do her necessity once she is on the plane. Kunuku was way too exited. I wonder if she knew something special was happening.

As I said my goodbye to her, I felt the tears welling up in my eyes. I told Jeff and Carole to go, before I really started to cry. The last 9 days had been quite emotional and I really got attached to her through it all. I know she is going to a good home and that comforts me.

When I got home the boys had to thoroughly search the car and see that indeed Kunuku was no longer here. "So, she's really gone then?" Angel asked. "Yes, she is. She is on her way to her new mommy." "Can we go to the beach now?" Nero asked, hardly waiting for me to finish my sentence. At times like these I don't even answer them; instead I just walked inside to tell Maya that the fire breathing dragon had left the building. She immediately got up and walked to the door. "Where do you think you are going, Miss?" I asked her. "To Jennifer" she said and sat there waiting for me to open the door. "I don't think so."

"I do!"

"You are not going anywhere until those paws have healed a bit more."

"Wanna bet?"

"Maya, you should know better. Mommy is bigger and stronger and you will just stay in this bedroom till I say you can go out."

"I will rip your bed to pieces!" she yelled at me, totally upset. I picked her up and as she sat on my arm sobbing I said "Let's see how your paws are tomorrow and maybe then you can go out okay?" She knew I was right. Her paws were not healed enough for her to go out of the house at all. She nodded sadly and said nothing. I held her for a while and as she started to fall asleep I softly put her down on the bed and left quietly. Poor thing, she still gets tired really quick.

The others came up to me to ask if indeed Kunuku was gone. They just couldn't believe it. Goofy was the last one to approach me on the matter. "Now that she's gone, we can focus a little more on the important things around here." I looked at him questioningly and said "like what?" "Like, this kitten. What's his name? Really mommy, if I don't put him on the list I can't guarantee a spot in the classroom when he's six weeks." This time instead of trying to explain things to him I just said "I don't know what his name is yet." Goofy looked at his list, looked at me with a frown and said "I'll put him under "kitten" then." I looked at his list and saw that in between a few names there were many "kittens" registered. Apparently cat mothers also have trouble finding a name for their kitten. "How do you know which kitten belongs to whom?" He scoffed at me and said "I know what I am doing here" and walked away. I just laughed and went to make milk for the little one.

As I sat there feeding him that night his name came to me: Vincent. His name will be Vincent. As I held Vincent out to Angel so he could clean him up after his meal, I said to him. "His name is Vincent. Do you like it?" He looked at me, then looked at the kitten and said "I think that name is perfect. You always find the perfect name Mommy." He's right, I do. I just wait a few days and the name just comes automatically. It's almost like magic.

Angel walked away and on his way bumped into Goofy "Have you heard Goofy?" I heard him saying behind me.

"What?"

"The little one is called Vincent."

"Really? When did this happen?"

"Just now. Isn't it a beautiful name?" Angel asked.

"It's okay, I like Goofy better" and he walked up to me. "So it's Vincent then, hmm?"

"Yes, Goofy, it's Vincent." I answered as he took out his list, scratched out one entirely different "kitten" and put Vincent behind it. He walked away, finally happy.

They are sometimes so funny. It's truly a joy having these animals around me. They help me in so many ways.

26.
Cactus juice

Ever since Kunuku has left, I have to say that Mozes is acting really weird. For the past few days he sleeps in the strangest positions and when he's awake he looks terrible. He has big bags under his eyes, which for a cat is just plain weird. When I call him to eat he says he's not hungry. But then at other times he's like a mad cat jumping and running around like crazy. At those times he's also very hungry and can eat two whole cans of cat food in a matter of seconds. Not that I give it to him, but he tries to steal the food away from the others. Dinner time is not fun at the moment.

I asked the others if they knew what was wrong with Mo, but they said they didn't know. However when they answered me they didn't look at me, as they normally do. That is how I know that they are lying. I had to find out what was going on here. This was definitely not normal. So for the past few days I've been keeping an eye on him.

I found out that he has been going to Bear's club a lot. And when he comes back from there he's like a zombie. I asked Bear what is going on in that club of his. "Why, is anything wrong?" he asked. "Well, Mo has been going to your club and when he comes home around eleven he looks like a zombie. What do you serve there?"

"Nothing in particular" he answered "just the regular cat milk, kibbles and stuff like that."

"Do you guys do some heavy partying then, that he's exhausted at eleven?"

"Why, no, the place doesn't get really going till three in the morning. It's completely dead at eleven… still."

"Then what is Mo doing there, that makes him come back like a zombie?"

"How should I know, I'm not his sitter" Bear said annoyed and walked away. I wanted to tell him that he had some responsibility to what was going on in his club, but he was gone before I could say a word.

So much for trying to find out what is going on through Bear. As I was thinking of a way to find out what is going on, Ari came walking into the room. "Aristotle" I said "just the cat I am looking for."

He stopped and looked at me "what is it, Mommy?"

"I need you to do something for me."

"It's going to cost you money" he said.

"I know it is, but it's worth it" he is such a little hustler but at times it can be very useful.

"I need you to keep an eye on Mozes. I want to know what he does at Bears' club."

"Okay, but we do have to make up a contract so I am sure that I will be paid."

"I don't need a contract. You can trust me to pay you!" And I really did not want a contract because before that would be ready we would be two weeks later.

"How do you know you will pay me?"

"You can trust me on my word?"

"Can I?"

166

"Yes, you can!"

"Well, I don't know, it's rather unusual to start any job without a contract. We cats have learned never to do business without a contract."

I sighed "how about I pay you half upfront and the other half once I know what I want to know?"

He thought about it for a few seconds and then nodded "Okay, Mommy, I will do it. Now give me the money." So I paid and he left. I have no idea where he was going, because the club did not open until 9.00 pm and it was three in the afternoon.

Two days later he came back to me with his findings "Okay, this is what I found out."

"Yes?" I said eagerly.

"At around 10.30 PM Mozes leaves the club and ten minutes later he comes back looking like a zombie. He is then kicked out of the club and staggers back home." He looked at me with pride of his detective work. I should have known to give more specific instructions. Already knowing the answer to my next question I still tried "what does he do in those ten minutes when he leaves the club?"

"I don't know." Ari said indignantly. He felt he had done such a good job, but it was not what I wanted to know.

"But that is what I asked you to find out Aristotle."

"You asked me to find out what he does at the club."

"I asked you to find out what he does that makes him a zombie."

"You said, and I quote" as he held his paws in the air making a quote mark "find out what Mo is doing at the club. I did just that. Pay up."

"I am not going to pay for a job badly done."

"See, I knew it!" he cried "Never do business without a contract."

Not wanting to give the entire human race a bad name, I said "okay, okay, I'll pay you. Can you find out something else for me?" I asked as I gave him his money.

He looked at the extra money that I was holding in front of him, as down payment for the next task. "Sure…" he said as he quickly took the money from my hand "what is it?"

"Can you find out what Mo does in those ten minutes when he leaves the club?"

"Oh yeah sure" he said and after a few seconds added "so you want to know what turns him into a zombie?"

I looked up at him and saw that he was smiling from ear to ear. That little sneak, he just conned me into giving him more money. He knew from the very beginning what I wanted to know. Before I could react he had already jumped off the table and ran away laughing. "I'll find out Mommy, don't worry" he shouted back at me.

It took him another three days to get back to me, but I know now. My Mo is a drug addict. Now you are probably thinking human drugs. Wrong! Cats have their own drugs and Mo is addicted to cactus juice. From what I could find out the cactus is cut and the juice extracted then concentrated in some way or the other. The more concentrated the better. Apparently it does not take much to give you a rush. Or in this case it will give a cat a rush. The dose has to be measured very carefully, and adapted to the weight of the cat otherwise it will be fatal. As you can imagine I was not happy with this news. "So how do we get Mo off his addiction?" I said to Ari. He looked at me and said "You only asked me to find out what he's doing. My work here is done. If you want to know more you can always hire me again." I gave him his money and said I would consider his offer.

Now it was up to me to find out how to get a cat off drugs. I wasn't going to ask any of my cats because they would probably not be very useful. I did what I thought was best. I locked Mozes in one of the bedrooms and not let him out at all. It was not a good idea, but the best one I had. I figured that keeping him off drugs for a week would get him sober again. Well it did, but it wasn't easy. He scratched, fought, attacked, vomited and also sometimes slept. It was a good thing I had moved everything out of the room before I locked him in there, because there would not have been a lot left standing.

On day 8 I walked into the room and I looked at my old Mo again. "What am I doing here?" was the first thing he asked me.

"I locked you in here." I said to him as I picked him up.

"Why, was I bad?"

"You don't remember anything Mo?"

"Not a thing."

"You don't remember going to Bear's club every night?"

"I never go to Bear's club."

"Yes, you did and you got cactus juice there."

"Bear doesn't serve cactus juice. It's very bad for you."

"Yes, I know that Mo. It is and you were using it."

"Noooooo, I wasn't!" he exclaimed.

"Yes, you were Mo."

"Can I have some food?" he said changing the subject.

"Sure you can, I'll take you to the kitchen."

I put him down and we walked to the kitchen, where the other cats were waiting for their breakfast as well. They all acted as if the drug addiction never happened, which just astonished me. I was at least expecting some lame remarks. They are always good at that when any of them does something stupid.

But I am afraid Mozes has suffered some permanent damage from this stuff. As he was eating, I was also feeding Vincent, and Mo looked up, looked at Vincent very closely and said: "That's one cute kitten. What's his name?"

I looked at him to see if he was kidding, but he wasn't.

"That's Vincent, Mo. He's been with us for two weeks now."

"Has he? I don't remember ever seeing him."

I decided not to make a very big deal out of it and just said "Vincent has been sleeping a lot because he is still so little, so maybe you were never around when he was awake."

Mo looked at me and nodded "That must be it" he said.

I just shook my head and continued with my work as cat mother. I really have the feeding nailed down now. It is such a joy to have such a small creature in your life. He is also starting to eat little bits. It's just so cute to see. It is so good for me in so many ways and I am thoroughly enjoying it.

I am just glad that Mo is off that horrible stuff and just hope that the memory loss or any other damage from the cactus juice is not something permanent. Now all that there is left for me to do, is repaint and redecorate that room.

27.
Vincent

Today I woke up and I saw that our waterbed had sprung a leak. The entire room was soaked but what was worse, the cushion I had in front of the litter box was also soaked and little Vincent was lying on it. I immediately grabbed him and walked with him into the living room. He was a little cold (from the air-conditioner) and not looking too hot. So I held him close to me trying to warm him up.

I don't understand how this happened. I woke up around 4.30 this morning and everything was fine. He was sleeping in his little bed next to me and there was no water anywhere. If it was there I would have noticed immediately. I woke up again at 7.00 and everything was wet. So he could not have been on that cushion for more than an hour. I mean it does take some time for it to become so completely soaked. It's not like the water pours out of the waterbed. He must have gone to the litter box and noticing the water when he came out he must have decided to stay on his cushion.

Around 7.30 I noticed he was having difficulty breathing. So I told my husband to call 911 and ask for the vet. We were figuring he would probably have pneumonia. The vet called back almost immediately and asked us to come to his office at 9.30. So we waited for two hours and all this time I held the little one close to me. It's so horrible that you can't do anything to help them.

At the vets office little Vincent got an anti-biotic shot. The doctor said that if he had an oxygen chamber he would have kept him there and put him in it. I was not really comforted with this statement; in fact it gave me an eerie feeling. Obviously the doctor was not to confident that Vincent was going to recover. I can now look at what he said objectively, but at that moment I only heard that Vincent was going to be fine.

We went home and I sat with Vincent for a few hours. He was obviously feeling miserable, and he was not sleeping at all. That had me worried so much. If he can't or won't sleep he'll never get better.

A little before two in the afternoon, I went to the bathroom and I left little Vincent on the couch. I came back five minutes later and saw he was lying rather strangely on his side. "Oh no!! Vincent!! VINCENT!!!!!" He had passed away in those few minutes I was not with him. I just sat there distraught, crying, not really knowing what to do. Why did I leave him?? My little darling.

Angel and Nero came up to me, to see what was going on. Angel gave little Vincent a nudge with his nose, I heard a sniff and I turned to look and saw one tear coming from his eye. After all, it was as much Angels' baby as it was mine. We sat there together when all of a sudden Angel lifted his head and howled! I guess it is his way of crying. I just sat there stroking my little baby, crying and Angel sat next to me.

We buried little Vincent next to Mickey.

In the evening I was sitting on the couch when Maya walked up to me and sat next to me. "I'm really sorry, Mommy" she said. I looked at her and asked her why she said that. Now she was the youngest again and she never really liked Vincent. "I know that Mommy, but I see how sad you are and that makes me sad." At that moment Luke jumped on the couch and said "same here, Mommy. I am sorry that you are hurting so much." They all came by, one by one, and told me how sorry they were. I hugged them. I love them all so very much. I hope they will all live forever, but I know that won't happen.

As for little Vincent, I never knew you could love a little creature so much in such a short time. Again a piece of my heart is missing and I am sure many more will follow.

I love you little Vincent and I will remember you always. Rest in peace my darling.

28.
The beach

I decided to dedicate one more chapter to the dogs. They really liked the first one and they were thrilled to hear about this one. Dogs are definitely different from the cats. I guess that is no big surprise to anyone, but I mean it in a different way of course. They are so much simpler. Clubby always made it clear that he had no respect for dogs. No good, simple-minded creatures he called them. "Can't have a decent conversation with them" was his statement when we took care of my mother's dog for a few months. Although I agree with the statement that dogs are simpler, I can't help but ask myself who is happier. They sleep, eat, play and thoroughly enjoy life. What more could you ask for? I wish my life was that simple! Of course they go to school. Just two years, mind you, and only 4 months per "school year". Compared to the cats that is really short. Cats also have 2 years of school but after that they can get higher education. That all depends on what they want to be, and can take 1 to 4 additional years.

Basically dogs have everything the cats have, but in simpler versions. In school they get lessons on "how to manipulate your owner" just like the cats do, but much less sophisticated. This means putting up sad faces, happy faces etc. Being boxers, my boys passed those classes with flying colors. Sad faces are their specialty. Nero is doing very well in running and Angel is on the wrestling team. Well, they were, they are almost 5 years old now so they left school 3 years ago. But you already knew that.

But in their school the dogs also had classes in subliminal messaging. At least that is what they called it. They love going to the beach. Going out for a walk is fine also, but the beach is their passion. Well here on Aruba we have the most beautiful beaches, but I don't take them where there are a lot of people. I go to the north side where it is a bit rougher, but quiet. Or to a little beach that hardly anyone knows. Now the beaches on the north side here are all smaller secluded bays. All the beaches names start with "boca". Boca literally means mouth. If my boys want to go to the beach they ask me if they can go to Boca Woof. Now of course Boca Woof doesn't exist but it's their general name for any of the beaches we ever go to. When I tell them no, they will sit near me, and start saying softly "we are going to boca woof… we are…" it really drives me nuts. Sometimes they will just come walking in, while singing "we are going to Boca woof" and then look at me to see if I get the message. The first time they did that I asked what they thought they were doing. Angel stopped his singing, looked at me and said "we learned that in school. The teacher calls it subliminal messaging. It's supposed to make you want to take us to the beach." I looked at him with my eyebrows slightly raised "trust me darling, there is nothing subliminal about what you are doing".

"There isn't?"

"No, not really. You can also just jump on my lap and say: let's go the beach."

"No, I can't do that Mommy, that would be rude."

"Okay, that would be rude, but this is not being subtle either."

Over the years they have tried all kinds of methods to get me to take them to the beach. Sometimes they would just walk up to me whenever I was sitting somewhere and put their front paws on my lap or shoulders, look straight at me and say "let's go".

"Excuse me?"

"You heard me, let's go."

"Go where?"

"Boca Woof."

"Now?"

"Yes, now."

"And if I don't?"

The funny thing, that question would always stump them. They wouldn't know what to say. And it would always be just one of them. They take turns at manipulating mommy. The other would be waiting by the side and when it wouldn't work the other one would always say "told you it wouldn't work".

"Oh yeah, well do you have a better idea?"

"Not yet, but I'm working on it."

There is that one time when they got me really angry. In some way or the other they had managed to get into the bathroom. I always hang my bathing suit in the bathroom to dry on the shower curtain rod and they had grabbed it. This time it was Nero. He's a little more daring than his brother. He walked up to me with my bathing suit in his mouth and dropped it in my lap and said "put that on and let's go swimming".

"Where did you get this?"

"From the bathroom. Now put it on and let's go."

"I don't think so. I don't really appreciate this" I said, looking at my bathing suit that now had two holes in it. Showing it to him I said "look what you did".

"Oops, sorry Mommy. I did not mean to ruin your bathing suit. But you can still wear it can't you?"

"I don't think so."

"You still have another one. Want me to get that one?"

"NO! I don't want you to get any bathing suit for me. We are not going anywhere!"

"Why not?"

"Because it's 9 in the evening. It's dark outside. We never go to the beach in the dark, remember?"

He looked at his brother, walked up to him and said "well, that was a brilliant plan. Why didn't you check the time?"

"I should check the time? Do it yourself." And they started arguing, so I stopped them. I told them that if they ever tried something like this ever again that we would never ever go to the beach again.

They stopped trying so very hard for a while after that incident but after a while they picked up on their subliminal messaging (they insist on calling it that) again. And it has remained their way of trying to go to the beach. Today they walked in again singing and looking at me to see if I get the message. I always get the message; I just choose to ignore it most of the time. But today was their lucky day, I decided I needed a break and really wanted to get out of the house.

They go absolutely nuts when I start packing for the beach. I always tell them to put on their swimming trunks. In their case it means their collars. At home they never wear their collars; I only put them on when we go out. They can hardly contain themselves when we go. When we get to the beach we always have to walk a bit before we get to the beach itself, so that is their time to run and play. Now don't get me wrong; we have a huge garden where they can run and play, but playing outdoors is obviously better.

When we get to the ocean, out comes the toy and that is when the real fun begins. The boys have an ocean toy. It looks like a tennis ball, but in a long tubular shape. Of course it floats and it is long enough for them to hold it together, which they always do. For some reason the toy has to be brought back to shore by the both of them. I always try to throw it as far as I can. When I bring my bathing suit I will sometimes jump in after them and race them to the toy. It is the best exercise I can give myself. I am a pretty good swimmer if I may say so myself, but these dogs are fast! And when I race them, I see that they try even harder.

Today I did not bring my bathing suit, so I just waited on the shore for them to bring the toy back. However there was one little snag. Nero was being a complete jerk. At all times he tried to keep the toy away from his brother. Angel was getting rather fed up with his brother's behavior as well and came crying to me.

"Mommy, Nero is not playing nice."

"I can see that, honey" I said, as I walked up to Nero to have a talk with him. I asked him what was going on, but he just looked away.

"Nero!" I said sternly "what is going on? Why are you not playing nice as always?" A low mumble was the answer this time. Maybe he was just in a bad mood? "Are you not feeling well?" I asked trying to see if the soft approach was perhaps the way to go. But again he did not answer but he did hang his head down. Nero is a bit of a challenge sometimes. He does not always listen that well and sometimes insists on doing things his own way. When I tell him to sit and stay he will do so, but always move to a spot which suits him better. He never has the patience to stay as he should and always slowly crawls or walks away.

Not really knowing whether I should be tough on him or not, I looked at him to see if I could figure out what was going on. In the meantime Angel was at my side, jumping and shouting "throw it then, throw it then" so I did just that. But the result was the same again. Nero did not want to share with his brother. So I cut our visit to the beach short this time.

As we drove home Nero was all normal again, at least as far as I could determine that. They sat in the back, nuzzling together as they always do when they return from the beach. I think they talk to each other about what they did, but I don't hear them say anything.

When I got home, I washed the sand and salt off and dried the boys off with a towel. They always like that. They love swimming, they hate being washed and they love being dried off. But when I water the plants they love to put their snout in the water stream or run through it, which of course gets them totally wet. Dogs are just weird.

When I was finished with them, I told them they were good boys and I walked inside to take my own shower. That is when the shit hit the fan. When I got to my room I heard growling and barking and as I ran outside to see what was going on, I saw Angel and Nero fighting. Now, never jump in between two fighting dogs: especially boxers who were bred as fighting dogs. I am convinced they can break my arm with one bite. So I ran toward the water hose, turned it on and turned it on them. At this point one of them was on the ground and the other had him by the throat. I did not see who was on top; I just kept on hosing them down. It took a few seconds to get them to stop, but it seemed like minutes. I hate it when they fight. They don't do it often. In all these years this was the third time they really went for each other.

After a fight it is important to establish who is the dominant one, which of course is me. I set them apart from each other and told them to stay. They know not to mess with me when I am really angry, but I have to be careful, because they are still angry with each other. I know that this fight was probably started by Nero, who had been in a bad mood all day. That is why I started with him.

I grabbed him by the scruff of his neck, shook him, pushed him to the ground and told him never ever to do that again. Well, actually I yelled at him. It is the only way to get through. As I looked into his eyes I saw his defiant look fading and knew that it was over. After that I walked up to his brother and did the same to him. Angel is never defiant as his brother is. He just sat there feeling sorry for himself. When I get really angry with them like that it really impresses them. After that I grabbed the both of them, stood over them to really make an impression and told them that there was only one boss in this house and that was me. "Now get out of my sight!" I said as I walked into the house and left them sitting there.

As I walked into the house I heard one of them say to the other "I'm sorry."

"I'm sorry too."

"Did I hurt you?"

"Yes, you did, my ear hurts."

"Well, let me see. It's still there"

"It is?"

"Yes, it is."

"Guess it's okay then."

I just shook my head and went to take my shower. I checked them for bruises after I was finished. Angel has a nasty bite behind his ear and Nero's head is a little bruised. They will survive. The first time they fought the damage was much worse. So much for another dog chapter. Never a dull day with these dogs!

29.
A legend

Today I received an e-mail saying that Clubby passed away. I sat behind my computer reading the e-mail and as the tears ran over my cheeks I remembered my dear Clubby. I remembered all the things he had told me about cats and their lives with humans. Now mind you it took me a few years to know all that I know now. He was not, what you would say, talkative; at least not about those things. Little by little I would get bits and pieces of information about how things worked in cat world.

I remember how he explained to me how not all cats can talk. Some of them never learn the human language, and in cat world they are considered stupid. I asked him if that word wasn't rather offensive and suggested that perhaps another word would be more appropriate. Turns out that calling a cat stupid is not offensive in the cat world at all. It is more a statement of a fact. Now if you think that it means that you can call your cat stupid, forget it. It only works from one cat to another. I made the mistake of calling one of mine "stupid" once and boy did they make me regret it. It took me days of kissing and cuddling before I was forgiven. And not just the one I had insulted, mind you. They were all insulted so I had to apologize to each and every one of them. A little detail Mr. Clubby failed to tell me about.

And then of course there was the time he told me about communication in general. The only other animals that master the human language are dogs. Cats and dogs can talk to each other in a human language, but they don't speak each others natural language. A cat cannot learn dog or vice versa. Now of course there will be a problem if the cat and the dog don't speak the same human language. Stray dogs only speak dog, which is why they constantly chase cats. I did not find that obvious at all, but I soon learned to accept certain things as a fact. Questioning cat logic will make your head spin and I stopped trying a long time ago. Now cats cannot communicate with any other animals. "But what if that animal lives with humans as well?" I asked him. According to Clubby, only dogs and cats can learn to master a human language. Other animals just don't have this ability. "So you can't ever talk to, hmm... let's say a horse?"

"How many times do I have to tell you? NO! Only cats and dogs have the ability to talk. All other animals are just too stupid. Well most dogs, are borderline stupid as well, but some of them manage it."

"But I don't think Sissy (our rabbit at the time) is stupid."

"Oh, you have to be kidding me?"

"Well, she figured out how to work the cat door sooner than you and Cindy did."

"That's because she rushes through with her head first while we cats like to inspect things that have been just installed."

"I have to disagree Clubby, we showed Sissy how it works and she caught on immediately. We showed you and it took you three days before you even started using it."

"Well, like I said, we cats tend to be a bit more careful. I mean, sure you can show me that it works but will it still work the next day?"

"That's not smart, that's just plain distrustful. Why would we install something for you to use if it were dangerous."

This conversation was not going in the direction he wanted, so he tried ending it by saying "Animals that can serve as food for us, cannot speak."

"So because a rabbit might be prey, it can't learn how to speak?"

"Yeah, you can't talk to an animal that could serve as your food, now could you? Imagine me talking to a bird just before I kill it." This got me laughing really hard and as the tears were flowing down my cheeks I said "You are so fat, you couldn't move fast enough to kill anything but an ant!" Needless to say that was the end of that conversation. Cats are easily offended and they have no sense of humor, or at least a good sense of humor.

I do admit that it was a bit crude of me to say what I did. Okay, Clubby was a bit fat, but he was still very fast. He could catch anything he wanted but honestly he was just too lazy to put any effort into it. I made it up to him by giving him something extra nice for dinner that night. That always made him smile.

But let's get back to the sense of humor of cats. Want to know about their sense of humor? It's just plain weird. They think putting a half dead mouse at your feet is fun. Clubby says that it's because humans react so funny. "That screaming is just hilarious" he would say "and the look on their face! Priceless!" They think that jumping on your belly, or even better on your face, while you are sleeping is fun. They think trying to trip you as you walk down the stairs is fun. Hitting you on the leg as you walk by... funny. Jumping out from behind the bushes, scaring you half to death... funny. Anyone who owns a cat can surely think of 100 more "funny" things that cats do.

And their best joke? Sitting somewhere and looking up rather intently and then when you come by and look to see what is there, they quickly move away. If that ever happens to you, listen closely and you may hear them snickering. They always do and because they think the joke is so good they can't always stay quiet about it.

I tried on several occasions to explain to Clubby that these things were not fun at all. We would always have fights about it. "Not funny!" "Yes, funny!" was a common heard argument in our house.

One time he actually scared the living daylights out of me. In our house we had an open staircase leading to the second floor. Underneath the staircase we hung our coats and there was a little cabinet for our shoes and other stuff. One day when I came walking down, something grabbed me by the leg. I saw two paws around my legs and then they were gone and I tried to see what it was but saw nothing. It all happened in a matter of milliseconds. I thought I was going to have a heart attack. I screamed and almost fell the rest of the way, but luckily I grabbed on and sat down, shaking terribly. Clubby came running up the stairs and started to lick my face. He was the one sitting on the cabinet and had put his paws around my leg. But he had pulled away in such a way that I could not see him anymore and it almost seemed as if a ghost had touched me.

"I'm sorry, Mommy" he kept saying as I was sitting there ash white, trying to recuperate. When I had regained my senses I said that I was fine. By the end of the day I could actually laugh about it, and it remained our little joke throughout the years. Whenever another cat would try a joke on me, Clubby would look at me and say "amateurs! Remember that day on the stairs, Mommy?" And indeed I did. I don't think I will ever forget.

There are just so many memories going through my head as I sit here crying over my Clubby. Clubby was a very intelligent cat. Before "that day" I would sometime take Clubby and Cindy out for a walk. We did not have our fence yet and our neighbor had a few nasty dogs. So in order to give them some exercise we walked them just like you would walk a dog. Clubby loved it. Cindy just made sure she stayed close to Clubby. He was her big hero and wherever he was, she wanted to be. Now whenever we would meet another cat, Clubby would never fight, or hiss, or make noises of any sort to that other cat. He would just stop and sit and look at that other cat. After a few seconds that cat would always run away. It always amazed me. Of course during the course of years I asked Clubby what that was about. He told me that when you get into your higher lives as a cat, you no longer need to fight in order to survive. What he did was just look deep into their eyes and there is something there that is recognized by other cats and makes them run off. He never told me what it was that these cats saw in his eyes.

As cats move on to their other lives, they get smarter and they pass their knowledge on to the younger cats. Younger cats in number of lives, that is. I once asked Clubby if he knew in which life he was now. He said he did but he never told me which one. I am guessing by what he told me it would be around 6 or 7. That means that he could still come back as one of my cats. He once told me that as they get on in cat lives they will choose people who need an intelligent cat. I never quite figured out what the requirements are. Who needs and who doesn't need to have an intelligent cat. Don't even know if it is a good sign or a bad sign. I thought my life was pretty good by the time Clubby came into it, so I comfort myself with the thought that it is a good sign. I guess I will never know for sure.

I can only say I am truly sad. Somehow I always thought I would see him again some day. I guess it teaches me that I should never put things off till tomorrow if I can do them today.

30.
Casper

Two weeks ago I received a phone call from the animal shelter, asking if I could take care of a kitten for a while. Of course, I said yes and that same afternoon I went to pick it up.

When I saw my new acquisition for the first time I was taken a little aback. At first sight he looked a little like Vincent and I felt a little pain in my heart. It was now almost three months ago since Vincent had passed away and I had not realized how much I still cared for him. Of course he came into my life at an especially difficult time. I guess it was only natural for me to still feel the pain.

But let's get back to the new kitten. As I picked him up I saw that he was almost completely white, except for the black curtain on his head (similar to the one little Vincent had) and his black tail. He had a few more black spots here and there, but for the most part he was white. It earned him the name Casper. Funny how sometimes it takes days to find a suitable name and sometimes it just comes to you almost immediately.

He's a cute little thing. At that time I am guessing he was 10 to 12 weeks and he is very affectionate. I took him home and introduced him to the rest of the family. Luke hissed at him, as he always hisses at any new kitten. Bear ignored him, looked at me and said "another one, Mommy? Don't you have enough?" I told him Casper was just visiting for two weeks. He scoffed and said "yeah, right!"

Maya, of course, was convinced that once again there is a little fire breathing dragon in the house. I told her to stop acting like a baby. That made her running from the room while yelling "you are a mean, Mommy!" Whatever! Sometimes they are just so spoiled, but I guess I am the one to be blamed for that.

I presume you know what Goofy's reaction was? That's right; he wanted to place him in school immediately. For once I gave in straight away. I figured that even if it was only for a short while, he would benefit from some schooling. Besides, Goofy can teach him some human. He doesn't speak any yet. Usually they start learning it at 10 weeks. But most of them have lessons before that. He has some catching up to do.

As I said that was two weeks ago and Casper is still with us and not going anywhere (as Bear predicted). So now we have 8 cats. But he will be the last one to come into the house for a while. But then again, it might be best not to say something like that. I know I will not be able to resist another poor kitten that needs rescuing. Call me a softy, but I just like cats and I will help whenever I can.

Come to think of it, except for Cindy and Mickey, all my cats were rescued in one way or the other. Cindy we got from a family as a companion for Clubby and Mickey was given to us by the owner of his mother. Because he was a half Cornish Rex and finally a cat with some pedigree I was more than happy to accept him. Aristotle, Bear and Goofy were born in our house, but I rescued their mother. She was wandering in front of our house very pregnant with obviously no place to rest and deliver her kittens. So I took her in and a week later she had the babies. They were quite overdue and it was a very difficult labor for her. We had named her Giselle. Now I have sat with our cat at home, when I was a child, many times when she was having kittens. I think I know by now a little how these things go, and how the kittens develop. Imagine my surprise when I checked on the kittens the next day and saw that their eyes were already opening. That is what happened with Ari. He opened his eyes the next day. Goofy and Bear started opening their eyes on day two. Talk about an overdue birth. Then there was Max. Also rescued from the street as a 6 week old kitten. Katinka rescued from my work and the only kitten that her mother had. Luke we found in front of our house, wandering in desperation after his mother had been killed by a car. The poor thing had no idea what to do. Maya, I almost ran her over as she tried to cross the street (No... Goofy did not really bring her home, but it's what I tell him). She obviously had no home to go to, which made me decide to take her home. Mozes, I found at my last job, the little pink rascal. Jimmy, we found in the bushes not far from our house where he was crying for his mother. The doctor said that if we hadn't found him that very day he would have been dead within the next few hours. He was incredibly skinny, underfed and in terrible shape and just six weeks old. Now he's just as fat as all my other cats. I guess I do a good job in feeding my cats. I don't know why all these kittens keep getting lost. But luckily I seem to find them.

But let's get back to our latest addition to the family. Little Casper is a fast learner. With the extra lessons Goofy is giving him, he is already speaking human quite well. But it's still a little "baby" talk and not quite comprehensible yet. Every now and then he comes up to me and starts talking. Quite frankly I don't get half of it. He also has a little lisp, which is making it even more difficult to understand what he is saying. It's cute though. I never had a cat with a lisp before. I asked Goofy if he should have special lessons to get rid of it. Or perhaps it would fade in time. Goofy said that he had no idea. He just had a kitten school, not some special education school. "Casper will have to make due with his handicap, just like any other cat" he announced to me in a rather rude way. "Goofy, I never asked you to give him special treatment" and I explained how I never had a cat with a lisp before and was just wondering if there were special courses for a cat like that, or for any cat with a handicap. If you want to call a lisp a handicap. I wonder if he also lisps when he meows? I most certainly won't hear the difference, I am sure. I asked Goofy and again he was very rude to me.

Now cats are never rude. At least mine have never been to me. So this was not like him at all and I asked him what was going on. "Nothing!" was his answer and he walked away. This time I wasn't letting this go away unnoticed as I do with so many things. I know by now when something is really wrong and this was one of those times. I ran after him and grabbed him off the floor. He struggled a little but I felt it was more for show rather than him really wanting to get away from me. I held him in my arms as I sat down and said "Tell me Goofy, what is going on?"

"Nothing."

"Yes, there is and I am not letting you go until you tell me."

"Oh rats Mommy, I don't have time for that."

"Well, then you better start talking fast."

He sighed heavily but finally said "I am a bit upset."

"About what?"

"You and Daddy?"

"Why is that?" But I must admit I knew what was coming.

"All the fighting is getting on my nerves."

Now it was my time to sigh. It was true. For the past months my husband and I have not been seeing eye to eye. I don't think that there was much yelling and actual fighting going on, but cats pick up little things like the tone of your voice. Yes, I would be a liar if I said that there hadn't been a lot of tension between the two of us.

He has been leaving the house a lot, which is fine by me. That way we won't fight that much or have arguments that will upset the "children". I also noticed that the dogs are not very comfortable. However this is a time when animals will not meddle in your life. They stay far away when their owners fight. They really get very upset when we fight. This is the case with every pet in every home all around the world. When the owners fight, they panic. Animals are very peaceful creatures for that matter. When they fight it's not about silly things as we humans often do. It's about serious issues, like honor and pride. If you call that serious issues. I guess we humans will laugh if someone will fight for things like that. At least some of us will. But they just get it on. Animals will not yell and scream at each other. They just go for the jugular immediately and get it over with. We humans have this tendency to keep harping on the same issues time and time again. Perhaps we should put on our fighting gloves at times as well and get it over with. On second thought, scrap that. Not one of my brightest ideas.

I looked at Goofy and was trying to figure out how I was going to explain this when suddenly he said "Can't you two make up like you always do?"As in any marriage we also had our share of fights in the past and we would always make up. That has not been happening lately. I guess the problem is more serious than I am willing to admit. "You know Goofy, sometimes the problems are so serious that they cannot be resolved so easily."

"Are you saying you guys are not going to make it up?"

"Well, we are trying to work things out, dear, but I won't make you any promises."

He did not look convinced so I asked him "but let me ask you a question. Why are you so upset by this? Normally you cats couldn't care less if we get along or not." Not to be rude to my cat, but it is true. As long as they get their food, they don't really care about anything else.

"True" he said "but it got to me because Daddy just left after you two argued, and I figured we weren't going to get fed tonight because you would be too upset."

I laughed "you will get your food tonight dear, don't worry. Mommy will always take care of you no matter what." I was glad to see that our fighting had not shifted the priorities of my cat. His main concern was still food!

31.
What is really important

In this entire book I've been talking about the cats and all their activities. The night club, the yoga lessons, the business deals, the schools and what not more. Now you may think that this means that cats have a life full of activity and education. But it's not really like that at all. It just seems so because cats can make any small thing seem like a big deal. But I must admit, at first I thought the same thing: that they were busy with all kinds of stuff and that all the sleeping they did all day was just distraction for humans.

Yesterday's talk with Goofy made me remember one of the first conversations I had with Clubby. It was one of those few conversations in which he talked a lot and actually explained some things. Normally he would assume all was logical and expected me to understand what was going on. Or as in that first conversation where he would answer everything with "yes" or "no". I can honestly tell you I did not understand most of what was going on and it often took me days of asking and probing and overhearing their conversations before I finally did find out what was going on. I realize that the last sentence makes it seem as if I had no life and was able to follow my cats around all day long. But the truth is that it's not that difficult to follow your cat around.

You see, they sleep most of the day. It's not a distraction at all. They really sleep 18 hours a day. Some sleep even more. I always made fun of Ari. Let me tell you something. You know how humans get bags under their eyes when they don't get enough sleep? Well Ari gets the same. His little eyes get all puffy and red and he just doesn't look good. He also gets really grumpy when he doesn't sleep enough. I would always joke about it and say that he needs 23 hours of sleep per day.

Now 23 hours is a little exaggerated but they do sleep approximately those 18 hours per day. That leaves 6 hours for their school, business, eating and everything else. They do part of this at night, or during the day when you are not at home. At least that is what mine did. During that conversation with Clubby, I was informed on how it really works.

"Tell me, how much time do you spend on your business?"

"Not much."

"And how much is that?"

"Couple of hours."

"A couple of hours per day? That is quite a lot."

"Who said it was per day?"

"Well, I just assumed…"

"You should never assume anything." Now bear in mind that this was my third or fourth real conversation with Clubby. The previous ones had all ended rather abruptly because I was asking "stupid" questions.

"I see. But could you be a little more specific in your answers? You see, I don't know everything yet. You must understand that I still have a lot to learn."

"I guess you are right. After all you are only human."

Now trust me when I say that for cats this means something completely different than when a human says it to another human. If a cat says "you are only human" they mean, you are stupid and ignorant and you could never understand how cats work anyway. I guess it's the same as with men never being able to understand women (or vice versa for that matter). But cats will never call you stupid and ignorant, because that would be rude.

"If you want to know you have to ask the right questions. Ask specific questions that I can answer with a yes or no."

"Do you work during the day?"

"Sometimes"

"Is your business going well?"

"I can't complain."

"Is Cindy your assistant?"

"I don't think you can call her that."

"Have you ever been sued?"

"Can't say that I have."

"Are cats monogamous?"

"That is not something that applies to us"

"Do you work 2 hours per day?"

"I don't think that is the exact amount."

"How old are you?"

"Not really a question I can answer with yes or no, can I?"

"Oh come on, Clubby. All questions I asked you could have answered with yes or no, but you didn't. Are you doing that on purpose?"

At that point he turned and looked at me with a big grin. Let me tell you, to see a cat smile at you is bizarre and you never get used to it. "I was just messing with you, Mommy" he said with a big giggle. "I do admire your determination in trying to ask the right questions."

"Well, thanks, I appreciate the compliment" I answered sarcastically.

"Don't be so sarcastic, Mommy. It's not nice." And that made me feel ashamed immediately. He was always able to do that. Whenever I was not being nice, or sarcastic he would point it out to me and made me feel ashamed.

"I know, but you really pushed your limit here."

"Yeah, I guess I did."

"So, why don't you just tell me how things work in Cat world, Clubby? If you tell me all at once, I never have to ask again." And those seemed to be the magic words.

He started explaining how cats do have their clubs, schools, businesses and what not more. They even have gyms. I thought that was hilarious; a cat going to the gym. However I did not want to stop Clubby from talking so I did not laugh and let him continue. They will spend a couple of hours on one or more of those things per day. Most of the time it will not be more than three hours, because the rest has to be spent on grooming, eating and harassing their owner.

Now school, for example, is not like we know it. Their system is that there is a kitten school for all kittens till 9 months. After that they have 2 years of "higher" education. One cat school year, lasts only six months, and those six months are spread out over one whole year (12 months). Now, whenever the head principal of the school does not feel like opening the school, it simply won't open. We humans would never accept such a thing of course, but for cats this is the most normal thing in the world. If not today, then tomorrow, is their attitude. You could, of course, argue that it's a good attitude and that we humans are completely nuts.

The same goes for the businesses, the cat doctor office, the clubs and everything else. Now the school does have tests that have to have a certain level, otherwise it is not valid. Of course I asked how it was possible to ever reach the desired level if you don't keep a schedule of some sort. To this he replied what made me think that there was no schedule. Of course there was a schedule and apparently all cats "know" this schedule. Don't ask me how; it is one of the secrets Clubby took to his grave. I did not really understand how this system was working, so as I kept on asking questions he finally answered "we cats work much more efficiently and effectively then humans." I could not help it, but all I said was "I see..."

"If you are going to be sarcastic again, I am leaving" he threatened me.

"I'm sorry Clubby, but I can't really picture cats being very efficient."

"Well, we are" he said, rather offended, but still continued explaining the cat world to me.

Cats can make decisions faster. Whenever there are meeting they come to a decision fast. The facts are presented and a decision is made. What he failed to mention and what I found out later, is that they change that decision a number of times afterwards. So much for efficiency. But cats have a short term memory when it comes to their own flaws. They have a very long term memory for everything you ever did wrong, but they have forgotten their own mistakes within 5 minutes, or less. Now don't try to remind them of it either. Worse mistake you can ever make.

I asked him if the schools take some sort of exams. And of course I had to know if they had advanced schooling. I mean how else can they have doctors? They do have exams and every cat always passes the exam. Now I don't really see how that can work. But according to Clubby, all cats are very intelligent and pass their exams. I did not dare ask if it might be a good idea to make the exams a little harder because I did not want him to stop talking. I was learning so much about their bizarre world and habits.

It basically boiled down to the fact that cats feel their world is perfect. We humans are just low creatures whom they tolerate in their presence because we are convenient. We pet them whenever they want it. We make sure they have a dry spot to sleep. Cats not only feel their world is perfect, but they are convinced they are perfect as well. They have no flaws whatsoever.

However on that day, Clubby did admit to me that cats have one weak spot. He made sure to explain that a weak spot is not the same as a flaw. What might that be you ask? It's food. Food is the weak spot of cats. It does not matter what happens. As long as there is food, cats don't really care what goes on. You can break down the house. There can be a huge fire. You may be on the verge of divorce. You may have just been to a funeral and be really upset or sad . Just make sure you feed your cat. It is really the only thing in this world they care about. Priority number 1 for cats is food.

Through the years I found this out so many times. When I came home from the operation on my thyroid, I was told by my cats that it was a good thing I left someone in charge of the food. I never got a "glad you're home" or a "does it hurt?" However when I got home I did get the question when dinner would be served. The next day they did realize it must have come across as a bit rude and they told me they were happy that I was home again, because it tasted so much better when I gave it to them. Sometimes they will be nice to you, but only because they know it will get them food. I was reminded of that yesterday when Goofy told me how afraid he was that dinner would not be served. For a moment there I thought he actually cared about the fighting, but food was still his main priority.

It was the longest conversation I ever had with Clubby that day. I learned so much more about their world during the following years and through lots of experience. At the end of our conversation Clubby did feel the need to tell me that if I ever divulged their weakness, I would regret it for the rest of my life. Well, I guess we will have to see about that, won't we?

32.
The nurse

Today Maya came home and announced that she is going to be a nurse. I looked at her and it reminded me of Cindy. Little Cindy also was a nurse. At least that's what she started out with and later changed it and became a beautician. I must admit I thought that being a beautician was also more suitable for Maya, so I asked her how she came to her decision.

She told me that she had been thinking about it ever since her terrible ordeal with the fire breathing dragon. I sighed, was she ever stop exaggerating about this? "What does a nurse cat do exactly, Maya?"

"Well, first of all it's a cat nurse."

"Of course it is."

"A cat nurse takes care of sick cats."

"You don't say."

"Yes, we do. The ones in the cat hospital need attending."

"There is a cat hospital?" This was the first time I ever heard of a cat hospital. I did know about the cat doctor, or doctor cat, whichever it may be, but I never heard of a cat hospital.

"Of course there is a cat hospital, Mommy."

I liked talking to Maya. She was the only one who would forgive me my stupid questions and just keep on talking. She never shows any signs of being annoyed at my stupidity. The thought did cross my mind at times that perhaps she just really liked talking so much so that she used my questions as an excuse to talk even more. But what do I care, right? She has a sweet voice and it's nice to listen to. That is why I enjoy the night time talks so much. Whenever she lies next to me and tells me all about her day, it is so soothing that I fall asleep really fast. And she falls asleep while talking as well which is just really cute.

But back to the cat hospital. I asked her what a cat nurse did in a hospital. You know that after all those years of talking to cats, you would think I would have learned something? Apparently I am too human. When Maya told me about becoming a nurse in a cat hospital, I got this image of a human hospital but the humans were replaced by cats. Of course I was wrong, very wrong.

I was imagining hospital beds for cats, with doctors roaming the hall way and nurses feeding the sick, dressing their wounds and giving everyone their medication or food, or both. I even went as far as imagining how they would wash the sick cats. Now be honest, wouldn't that be the way you would imagine it? It is the way I imagined it, but it is really very simple.

The hospital is really just a shelter where cats come together. There are no beds, no doctors, no medication, nothing really. Just cat nurses and their tasks basically consist of two things. The first one is to sit and listen to the complaining of the cats that come there. The second one is to clean any wounds that these cats may have. Now I can honestly tell you that I had my doubts about both these tasks and Maya's suitability for the job.

The first one got me wondering because Maya really likes to talk so much herself. I asked myself how much of a good listener she would be. Most talkers are not listeners, is my experience. Second, I did not really see Maya cleaning wounds of other cats. Instead of telling her about my doubts I asked her how she had come to the decision to become a nurse. She told me when she was so terribly injured, from her encounter with the fire breathing dragon, it got her thinking about what she wanted to do with her life. She realized how nice it would have been if someone else had been licking and cleaning her paws for her. That made her decide to become a cat nurse. "Because, let's face it, Mommy" she ended her explanation "you weren't much help back then."

"Excuse me? I think I did a pretty good nursing job."

"You did okay... for a human."

"Well, thank you very much. But what did you expect me to do? Lick your paws?"

"It would have helped."

"So sorry, to tell you this Maya, but I do my nursing the human way, not the cat way."

"So I noticed."

"Well, if my nursing wasn't good enough, why didn't you go to the cat hospital?"

"I never said it wasn't good enough. It sufficed, but it was... how shall I put this... human."

"You did not answer my question. Why didn't you go to the cat hospital to get proper treatment?"

"You kept me locked up, remember? And by the time I got to go out again I did not need it anymore."

I knew I was never going to hear the end of me locking her up, so I was thinking of a way to cut this conversation short when Casper came running up. He jumped on the table. He is a funny cat and one that is not too careful. Most of the time when he jumps on the table he comes at it with such speed that he slides off the table again at the other end. It always makes me laugh, but this time Maya was sitting there and he bumped into her. Now Maya doesn't like Casper too much. According to her he is an "annoying little boy" and she ignores him most of the time. Casper on the other hand is completely wild about Maya and follows her around everywhere. Of course he wants to play with her all the time. Not only with her, but with anyone who is willing to play. Sometimes Mozes will indulge him. Bear, Goofy and Ari are just too plain old to play with such a bundle of energy. After all they are nearly 15 years old. I must say, they don't look their age. In human years they would be 105. I can only hope to look that good when I am 105.

Of course Luke will only play with the dogs. Jimmy isn't very sociable either. He's a weird one that Jimmy, by the way. So that leaves only Maya to play with and she doesn't like it. It is my opinion that Maya overreacts a little when it comes to Casper and she did so today as well. After she had recovered from the bumping incident, she turned around and smacked Casper on the head.

"Maya! That is not nice" I said to her.

"He bumped into me."

"I know he did. It was an accident, Maya."

"He always does these things." She was starting to get upset now because I was defending Casper.

"He is still a young kitten Maya. What can you expect?"

"I expect him to behave!" She was almost hysterical at this point.

"Maya, Maya" I said as I picked her up in order to calm her down a little "don't you remember what you were like when you were a kitten?"

She looked at me, terribly angry for the fact that I was not going along with her antics. "You bumped into the bigger cats as well" I said, trying to remind her of her days as a kitten. "I can ask Goofy how much of a pain in the butt you were as a kitten." That did the trick, as she calmed down considerably.

"I was never a pain in the behind, Mommy" she said in a rather lofty "I was always adorable."

"Yes, you were, dear" I said smiling and added "you were an adorable pain in the behind."

It did not surprise me that this was the last straw. She wriggled free from my arms and walked away terribly offended. I looked at Casper and shrugged. Maya was always easily offended. She expects to be treated like a little princess at all times. While she gets away with it most of the time, there are moments when I will have my fun with her. It's only fair that I get to tease my cats once in a while. That way I can get some payback for all the trouble they put me through.

Casper looked at me and said "Sjo we are not going to play then?" (Did I mention he had a lisp?) "I guess not, Casper."

"Oh sjoks, that sjucks." Now I know I am not supposed to laugh, but I just can't help myself. You see all these cats have a meticulous enunciation. They pride themselves on speaking "correctly". But little Casper has a lisp and he is trying to speak correctly as well which makes his lisp even worse. I tried to explain to him not to think about it too much. It didn't help too much.

And the worse part? For some reason he always finds words with an "s" in it. I tried to find him synonyms for most of them, but he refuses to use them.

"Yes it does, honey. But what can you do huh?"

"Sjall we go and play, Mommy?"

"What would you like to play honey?"

"Hide and sjeek."

"Okay, you want to hide or seek?"

"No, hide and sjeek."

"I know, would you like to hide or seek?"

"Sjorry, Mommy, but it's hide and sjeek."

"I know. Would you like to go hide and I find you or will I hide and you find me?"

"Oh, I sjee! You want to know if I want to hide or sjeek?"

"Exactly."

"Let me sjee… I think I will hide. I have the perfect sjpot"

"Okay, Casper. I will come and find you soon" and off he went to his hiding spot.

Playing hide and seek with cats is the easiest game in the world. You just make sure they are the ones hiding. That is not hard because they always want to hide. They will never say "I think I will seek" or "sjeek" in Casper's' case. I don't know why, but they never do. They do, however, like to give the impression that they thought about it. But anyway, they will always hide and you can just sit and do nothing. It's not like they expect you to go searching for them anyway. They will fall asleep on their hiding place, which is always their favorite sleeping spot. After an hour or three/four you just walk up to them, wake them up and say "found you!" They have no idea that a couple of hours have passed, since cats don't live by the clock. It's the easiest game in the world and the only one I am actually good at.

33.
Meetings

As I mentioned earlier, cats have meetings. During those meetings decisions are made. Important decisions such as if they will tease me today or annoy me. It doesn't make a big difference because I usually get pretty annoyed when they tease me. I get really annoyed when they annoy me.

But Bear organizes different kinds of meetings. For some reason he feels that it is his task to guard the house. So what he does is patrol around the yard and takes notes of all that is out of place. He then holds a meeting in which he shares his findings with the other cats. I will give you the meeting that they had this afternoon.

"Today at zero 900 hours I noticed that there were paw prints in the back of the yard that do not belong to any of us."

No reaction from the other cats.

"Did any of you see the intruder that came into our yard?"

Still no reaction from the other cats.

"Luke, did you invite some friend over?"

Luke gives him the silent treatment.

"Goofy. Any of your kittens that were getting extra schooling?"

"When?"

"This morning at zero 900 hours."

"When?"

"This morning at zero 900 hours" Bear replies again but a little louder.

"Yeah, yeah, I heard you the first time. I have no idea what you are saying."

"This morning at 9" Ari always feels the need to explain things.

"What happened this morning at 9?"

"You gave lessons to a kitten" Maya explained since she had been silent way too long.

"I don't think so."

"Yes, you did, Bear found his paw print in the yard" Maya again, taking her opportunity to talk.

"I never said it belonged to one of Goofy's students, I just asked if he gave any kittens schooling today."

"Since when are you interested in my students?"

"I think he is interested in that one that came to our house" Maya once again felt the need to open her mouth.

"I am only trying to determine who that paw print in the back yard belongs to" I could hear Bear getting annoyed now.

"How can you know it is from one of Goofy's students?" This time it was Mozes asking a question.

Bear: "I don't."

May: "Then why do you blame Goofy?"

Bear: "I don't blame Goofy."

Mozes: "Yes, you did, you said it was the paw print of one of his students."

Bear: "I never said such a thing."

Maya: "Well, I sure heard you asking Goofy if he gave lessons."

Goofy: "Of course I give lessons, everyone knows that."

Maya: "Yeah, everyone knows that. Why do you ask Bear? Are you getting senile?"

Bear: "Of course I know Goofy gives lessons. I just…"

Goofy: "Then why do you have to ask me if I do?"

Bear: "I only wanted to know if you gave some kittens lessons this morning."

Goofy: "Why?"

Bear: "Because I want to know if that paw print is his."

Maya: "It could be a her as well."

Jimmy: "No it can't. Girls are stupid, they don't go to school."

Maya: "Yes, they can. I go to school!"

Jimmy: "Well then maybe it is your paw print."

Bear: "It's not Maya's print. I know what all your prints look like."

Maya: "Really?

Bear: "Yes, I do."

Maya: "Did you get special training for that?"

Bear: "Not really, I learned it all by myself."

Maya: "Wow! That is so great."

Bear: "Why, thank you Maya."

Luke: "Can we all go to sleep now?"

Bear: "Not until we know to whom that paw print belongs."

Maya: "It was Goofy's student."

Goofy: "What student?"

Bear: "The one that came here this morning?"

Goofy: "There was no student here this morning."

Maya: "Then why did you say there was?"

Goofy: "I never said that."

Jimmy: "Yes, you did. You said it was his paw print."

Maya: "I still think it was a girl."

Jimmy: "I told you girls are stupid."

Maya: "Well so are boys!"

Bear: "Okay, stop it right now!"

For a few seconds everyone is silent.

Luke: "You know what... I am going to sleep."

Bear: "Not until I finish this meeting."

Ari: "There is more then?"

Bear: "Yes, there is."

Mozes: "Like what."

Maya: "Yeah, like what?"

Bear: "Well I would like to know who decided to leave the yard through the side fence today."

Maya: "Are we not allowed to go out of the yard through the side fence?"

Luke: "Of course we are. He is just trying to bully us."

Bear: "I never said you are not allowed to leave through the side fence. I just wanted to know who did."

Ari: "Why?"

Bear: "Because I noticed that there were paw prints in front of the fence."

Luke: "I thought you recognized our paw prints?"

Bear: "I do."

Ari: "In that case you don't have to ask who was there. You already know."

Maya: "Did you lie when you said you could recognize our paw prints?"

Bear: "Of course I didn't."

Luke: "Well I think he was just bragging about that."

Bear: "I was not!"

Ari: "Honestly Bear, if you knew you wouldn't be asking it."

Poor Bear, I guess he asked the wrong question. I have no idea why he asked it anyway and why it would matter who went out of the side fence, but I guess he had his reason. Sometimes I listen in on these meetings and I am glad to always find out that what they do to me, namely drive me crazy, they do to each other as well. The only problem is that they don't really get upset about it and just keep on talking or changing the subject as they please. In the beginning I wanted to make sure that the conversation made some sense. After all these years I still try that at times, but now I know that I will never be able to. So why try, you ask? Just for the fun of it.

Funny thing though, if I try to change the subject of the conversation the way that they always do, they won't accept it. They always come back to the same subject. I once asked Ari why that was. He walked away. So I said to him that he didn't know the answer. He turned around, looked at me and said "you wouldn't understand the answer."

"Try me Ari. You might be surprised. I am not a complete idiot."

"Mommy, trust me, I've known you for 15 years now and I know you still don't get us cats. There is no way ever that you are going to understand the answer."

"I think you are just saying that because you have no answer."

"Don't go there Mommy."

"Why not? You guys always do the same thing to me."

"This conversation is over!"

"Cat!"

"Human!"

34.
Retiring

Bear and Luke have been having a lot of conversations these days. I was wondering what they were talking about all the time. As it turns out Bear is thinking about selling the club. He says he is getting too old to run it properly. So he approached Luke to see if he wants to take over the club.

But Luke is hesitant. He doesn't know if he has the skills and knowledge to run a club. So he came to me for advice. I was honored by the fact that he came to me for advice. I was also a little anxious. To say that my career as a cat consultant was a successful one is the understatement of the year. Each and every time the ending of the conversation was "that is the most ridiculous thing I ever heard" or something in that area. Depending on the cat, the statement was bad or even worse. All I did was tell them what I would do if I were a cat. I think that there lies the problem. Besides don't they have consultant cats for that?

It may have become obvious by now that while I have been talking to cats for many, many years, I still have no idea what makes them tick. We live in peaceful coexistence and that's where it ends. For them it is easier to make it clear what they want. If they are feeling ill, or sad, or if they are hurt, hungry, happy, they can tell me about it. It makes things a little easier... for them. Well I would lie if I said it didn't make things easier for me. If I tell them to get lost, I know they understand me. It doesn't mean they listen any better though.

But I am getting sidetracked again. As I said, Luke came to me for advice on the whole club business "Mommy, what do you think I should do?"

"About what, dear?"

"Should I buy the club from Bear or not?"

"Do you have the money to pay for it?"

"Yes, I do."

"Is it something you would like to do?"

"Yes, I would."

"Then what is the problem?"

"I don't know if I can."

And there I got stuck. I believe that if you want something really bad you will find a way in which you can achieve your goal. How many times have I not learned things just by doing them? But I was hesitant telling Luke that. With my experience on consulting my cats, this would be an answer for a human and not for a cat. While I sat there looking at Luke and thinking what I would answer him, Luke was looking at me in wonder why I had not said anything.

"Hello? Are we going to say anything Mommy?"

"Yes, we are dear. But I am thinking about what to say."

"Must be difficult for you."

"What must be difficult?"

"Thinking."

"Not in particular."

"Well, if it's not, then why is it taking you so long?"

A couple of years ago I would have been offended by something like that, but I've been hearing such remarks for many years now. They don't really mean anything by it. They just say what they think and blurt it out. It's the way they talk to each other as well. Because it does not offend them when they say such things to each other, they do not realize that they might offend you with any of their remarks. Besides, they are not really willing to adapt their ways for humans. They are perfect the way they are, as we all know. Fortunately for Luke I am wiser now, otherwise I would have walked away.

"I want to make sure I am giving you the right answer."

"There is no right or wrong answer."

"Of course there is."

"No there's not."

"Do you want to hear what I have to say or not?"

"Only if you thought about it long enough" he replied sarcastically. At that point I decided to do something I've never done before; be mean.

"If you think that you can't do it, then you should not do it."

"Why would you say something like that?"

"Because, you said you don't think you can do it. Then don't do it."

"But it is your job to tell me that I can do it."

"No it's not; you asked me what I think you should do."

"And you should tell me to do it."

"But you said you don't think you can do it."

"Well, maybe I am just insecure."

"You can't run a business when you are insecure."

"Aren't you ever insecure when it comes to your business?"

"Of course I am, but I never say that I can't do it. Thinking you can't do it and being insecure are two completely different things."

"So you think that I can do it?"

"Did you hear me say that?"

"Why would you think that I can't do it?"

"It does not really matter what I think. It matters what you think and you think that you can't do it."

"Of course I can do it! I am going to Bear right now and tell him I will buy his club. I will show you! Telling me that I can't do it…" he mumbled as he walked away to find Bear.

I sat there in amazement. I wanted Luke to take over the club because I think he will be great at it. However in the past in such a situation I always said to my cats that they should do it and they always backed out because my advice "sucked". Was this the way to go? Was this really my first time as a cat advisor with a positive ending? I did not hear the words "that is the most ridiculous thing I ever heard" at the end of this conversation. I was actually stunned. After all these years, I finally managed to do something right by my cats? Sure took me long enough. As I was sitting there still wondering if I indeed had done the right thing, Bear walked up to me.

"Thanks, Mommy."

"For what, honey?"

"For getting Luke to buy the club from me."

"You guys closed the deal?"

"We sure did. Just now, and I can still do my one cat show."

"That's good to hear, Bear. I am glad for you and Luke."

"That must have been some advice you gave him."

"Well, I don't know about that."

"It was. Luke told me that it was the best advice he had ever gotten."

"You know me Bear, I always try to help." I was really amazed and tried not to show it.

"Yes, you do Mommy. Now we are letting Ari draw up the contract and then we are finished."

"Bear?"

"Yes Mommy?"

"Is that a good idea? Letting Ari draw up the contract?"

"Why not, he is an expert at drawing up contracts."

"That is exactly what I am afraid of and he will probably charge you guys a lot of money for it."

"Oh, Mommy, One shining moment of success and then it's back to your old self, isn't it?"

"Excuse me?"

So Bear explained to me that going into business with Ari and let him draw up the contract at such a point was not a good idea. However for drawing up contracts between two independent parties, Ari was the best. I never knew that about my Aristotle. All I know about his business dealings is that he's a schemer. Another thing I never knew about my cat. Even after 15 years, they still amaze me. At least I had this one little success with Luke and they are never taking that away from me. Perhaps there is a future for me as a cat advisor after all?

35.
Moving out

A few weeks ago my husband moved out of the house. Things had not been going well between us for quite some time and this was just another step in our way toward divorce. I cannot say I am truly upset about the entire situation at this moment. Of course when the subject of separation came up I was very sad. You don't start a life together thinking that at some point you will end it. However the weeks before he left were very stressful and that is why I can now say that I am not very upset about it. Things like this happen in life and the only thing you can do is deal with them the best that you can.

However what amazed me was that none of the cats or dogs asked anything about it or commented on the situation. I was starting to wonder if they had even noticed when Bear came up to me today. He sat in front of me on the table and looked at me really serious. "Mommy, there is something I have to tell you."

"Yes, dear?"

"Daddy hasn't been home for weeks now" he said in a really dark voice. I couldn't help but laugh and said "I know that, Bear." I could see that he was taken totally by surprise and said "You mean, you knew about this?"

"Of course I knew. What do you think? He would move out and I would not notice?"

"Well, I didn't. But I realized that I hadn't seen him for some time." Turns out he had discussed it with the other cats during one of their meetings and all of them had agreed that it had been a while since they had last seen Daddy. "We noticed it last week" he told me.

It was clear to me now why none of them had said anything about it. They thought I hadn't noticed and would be upset if I found out. I smiled and patted him on his head. "Don't worry, Bear. Mommy knew that Daddy moved out." He looked at me relieved and left. Must be nice to be able to accept things so quickly. We humans have much more problems accepting new situations. I was expecting to have long discussions about how and why.

Aristotle told me that last week they had a long discussion on how they would tell me "it". He explained to me how the task fell on Bear since he was the one who brought it up. "But he was supposed to tell you the day after the meeting and not wait a week" He said rather upset. I told him that it did not matter and that I knew it all along. And then he said something which really surprised me "I must say Mommy, you have been much nicer during these past few weeks." I looked at him and thought for a minute. I do know that when I am a little stressed I can't tolerate that much from these cats. I am more likely to be grumpy when they ask me something when things are not going well. I cannot say that my husband and I were constantly arguing. Our china did not suffer because of the separation. We did fight at times, but I guess that is normal when you are in the situation that we were in. Apparently the whole situation was having a mayor impact on me. I suppose it is logical, I just never realized it was that bad.

Truth is that ever since he moved out I have been more at ease, I sleep better and I feel better. Makes you wonder in what shape your marriage was, if you feel so much better so soon after separating. I guess it was pretty bad. In that case the choice is all the easier. Now all I have to do is make sure to let him know that I want a divorce. It was the intention for this separation period to see if either of us wanted to continue this relationship. Seeing how I am feeling, I guess my decision has been made.

I thanked Ari for pointing out that simple fact to me. He looked at me in a puzzled kind of way and said "don't you know how you act?"

"Of course I do. But I thought I was acting the same all the time."

"I can tell you Mommy, you were not acting the same."

"Yes, thank you dear. I did not realize there was such a big difference."

"I just told you there was a big difference."

I sighed and walked away, but he came after me.

"Don't try to avoid this conversation, Mommy."

"I'm not. It's just that I don't know how to make it clear what I mean."

"You just say it."

"It's not that simple."

"Yes, it is. You just say, I was acting stupid and did not know it."

"But I wasn't acting stupid. I was just a little grumpy."

"Oh trust me Mommy. You were acting stupid."

"Thank you for pointing that out to me Ari. Now leave me alone."

"Typical human!"

"Whatever!"

We often end our conversations like that. Ari can be a little difficult to talk to at times. He will keep insisting on continuing a certain subject and when you don't want to continue the conversation he will accuse you of avoiding the discussion. At some point I will tell him to leave me alone, at which point he will tell me I am a typical human. But then again how much of a typical human can you be when you talk to your cats?

I mean, Clubby was the most intelligent of them all. And I was able to talk to him in a sort of normal way. But even then I would have to carefully choose my words. They will take anything literally and there is no way to stop it. Then they will keep on asking about it until they drive you absolutely mad. As long as the conversation is about food, feeding times and sleep, you are safe. Anything beyond that is at your own risk.

I still remember one of those conversations very well. It was with Cindy. I don't really remember how the conversation started or even what we were talking about but at a certain point I said "you have to cut your coat according to your cloth".

"Why would I want to cut my coat?"

"You don't. It's just an expression."

"And cats don't wear clothes."

"Excuse me?"

"We don't wear clothes."

"I know that."

"Then why do you want me to wear clothes?"

"I never said I wanted you to wear clothes."

"And you said to cut my coat. Why?"

"I never said to cut your coat."

"You said I should cut my coat and wear clothes. I will be cold if I cut my coat."

Trying to be funny I answered "that's where the clothes come in handy."

"So you do want me to wear clothes."

"It was a joke, Cindy."

"Not a very funny one!"

"I never said that you should cut your coat. I used an expression and you just misunderstood me."

"Oh, so now you are saying that I am stupid as well."

"Misunderstanding someone doesn't mean you are stupid. It can also mean that the other person was not successful in getting their message across."

"So you are saying that you are stupid?"

"No, I am not."

"Well if I am not stupid and you are not stupid, how come we don't understand each other?"

I had many responses to that question, but kept them to myself since I did not want to aggravate her anymore. She looked at me and said "I think it's because you are human."

"I think so too, dear" I said and walked away.

I guess many, if not all, of my conversations with my cats end up with either one of us getting up and leaving. It's the way of life, I guess. I think that I will have to accept two things: first of all that my marriage is over and second that I will never be able to have a normal conversation with my cats. After 15 years you think I would know that by now. But sometimes the conversations are almost normal. Then I think that I am finally "getting" them. But I never do. Oh well, live and learn.

36.
Fighting

Today when I woke up I walked into the kitchen to find out that Luke had been fighting again. The side of his neck and his cheek were all covered with blood. After some closer investigation it looked worse than it was. There was a lot of dried blood and after cleaning that off it sure looked better. He had a few nasty scratches on his cheek, but nothing so serious that he has to go to the doctor.

Needless to say while cleaning there were loud protests from Mr. Red himself. I told him that the more he cooperated, the sooner I would be finished. But cats don't listen to rational. Maya was there of course offering to do her duty as cat nurse (or was that a nurse cat?). So I stopped my work and for a moment there I thought he was going to let her. But he jumped of the kitchen counter and walked to my bedroom, leaving Maya behind, very disappointed. He sat in front of the door waiting for me to open it. I let him in and as he installed himself on the bed I just looked at him. "What?" he said when he saw I was watching him. "Why did you fight, Luke?" He turned away and pretended that he was very tired.

There is one thing I have learned in all those years and that is to see when they are avoiding something. He was not tired at all. Luke was avoiding answering my question so I knew there was something going on. I poked him in his side and said "What's going on Luke." He continued to ignore me and I continued to poke him. Not hard, mind you. I never hurt my cats. If they are bad they get a pat on the behind. I don't even think they feel it, but it's more the humiliation that will get to them. So there I was poking my cat and he was ignoring me. I knew this was a matter of who had the longest breath and in this case I was determined to be the one.

After about 5 minutes, Luke jumped up and said "enough already!"

"Tell me what is going on Luke and I will stop."

"You don't want to know."

"I do want to know."

"Why?"

"Because I have a feeling that it's important."

"How can you know that?"

"Intuition… Experience… Fingerspitzengefühl… you name it."

"What do your fingers have to do with it?"

"My fingers have nothing to do with it. Don't try to change the subject."

"I'm not, you are. You are the one starting about your fingers."

"Yes, I did and if you don't start talking soon, I will start poking you again with this finger" I said as pointed my index finger at him.

He gave me a nasty look but I could see that I had won. It was all a matter of waiting for him to start talking. It took him a long while to gather his thoughts and start talking. That is not like Luke at all. Most of the time he knows exactly what to say. The subject of the fight in this case was me. Apparently the cats in the club have been making fun of the fact that my cats are now being taken care of by a "single human". I asked Luke what difference that made. He looked at me with great shock in his eyes. "Are you kidding me?" he asked. Being raised by a single human is the most humiliating thing for a cat. I asked him how that could be, since many humans who live alone have cats. "Yes, but they start out that way" he cried at me. I sighed and told him to calm down. I really had no idea what this fuss was all about. So he explained it to me, in his usual cat like way which makes it necessary for me to ask a gazillion questions before I finally found out what it was all about.

For cats it is very humiliating when their owners split up. Yeah, I know, it sounds ridiculous, but Luke was really upset about it. Now if you are a single person who owns a cat that is not a problem. But when cat parents split up it is apparently a big deal for the cat. I told him that I thought he was exaggerating just a tad, since they at first did not even notice that we split up. That was not the point, Luke told me. I really did not understand where the problem was here. First they had two owners and now they only had one. If any of them wanted to go live with Daddy I had no problem with that. As he was talking and explaining it to me, I got the feeling that us splitting up was not really the issue here. So I kept on asking and asking.

I also wanted to know why he had been fighting. Doesn't seem to me like it would be something you would fight over with strange cats. All I got from him is that he was defending my honor in that fight and after that everything he said got more and more incomprehensible with every word he uttered.

I left the room and decided to ask the other cats what was going on. Ari is always a good cat to ask these things. I called him and thinking he was getting some food, he came running, together with Bear and Goofy. Funny, whenever I call one cat three or more show up. Heaven forbid you give something to one and not the other. "Ari, I need to talk to you" I said as he showed up. "Whoa, you are all on your own bro" Bear said as he turned around and got out of the room as fast as he could. Goofy just sat there wondering why there was no food.

Ari sighed and said "what is it, Mommy" in a very bored tone.

"I need to know why Luke was fighting."

"Didn't he tell you?"

"He's not making any sense. Just some incomprehensible gibberish."

So once again I heard the same explanation on how it was unbearable for cats when their owners split up. I looked at him and said "would that be a reason for you to start a fight with another cat?"

"No. Not really."

"Well, then I don't buy that explanation. In fact I think you guys are making it all up. Why was Luke fighting?"

He sighed and looked around to see if he could find some back up from one of the other cats. Unfortunately for him there was no one around. I told him that I did not believe that owners' splitting up was so humiliating for cats and that there was something going on that they were not telling me. Again he looked around to see if someone was there to help him. By this time he was lucky because Maya had just walked in. "What are we talking about?" she asked. "Nothing" Ari said. He obviously did not want our little chatterbox to be part on this conversation. "Yes you are. You are talking about something."

I told Maya that we were talking about Luke and his fighting and as I was saying that I could see Ari getting upset. "Luke shouldn't take things so personally" Maya said.

"What do you mean by that?" I asked.

"She means nothing by that" Ari said quickly and sat in between Maya and me. "Don't speak for me, Ari. I think Mommy should know what is going on."

"I tend to agree with Maya on this one Ari,"

"Okay, so fine, just don't say I did not try to warn you."

Maya started explaining that the other cats had been teasing Luke. They had been telling him that I was going to get a new Daddy now and this would mean that he would be moved out of the house as would all the other cats. I was surprised and asked them why they would ever think something like that. "Well, are you not going to get a new Daddy for us?"

"Not at this moment."

"But some time you will."

"I don't know if I will."

"But you will fall in love again some time in the future."

"Perhaps I will, but perhaps I won't."

"But you could meet a wonderful new Daddy and live with him."

"That is very possible but not really an issue at the moment, is it?"

I was getting rather tired of this beating around the bush, so I said that they would just have to tell me directly where this was going. I even threatened not to feed them tonight. That always helps. Ari decided that he would be the one to tell me. "We are afraid that you will find someone and fall in love with him and then you will forget all about us and then we will have to move out because you are not feeding us anymore and then we will starve to death and when that happens we will all die…" I stopped him talking by putting my index finger and thumb on his nose and chin and shutting his mouth that way.

"Will you stop talking for just one second Ari" I said to him and he nodded, so I let go.

"Is this why Luke started fighting with those other cats?" Ari and Maya nodded in agreement. I sighed, what a ridiculous reason to fight. I explained to them that at this moment I had no intention of finding a new Daddy, as they called it. "I have no intention of looking for a new Daddy either for that matter." I continued explaining that while in the future there always is the possibility that I might meet someone I will really like and perhaps even fall in love with, but that I was not looking for that person. "If I meet that person, it will happen and not sooner" I know that it made absolutely no sense to them, so I tried a very simple approach. I told them that if there was ever going to be a new Daddy, then he would have to accept my cats as being part of my life. This seemed to calm them down considerably.

"So we are not going to starve to death?" Goofy asked. He had been sitting there the whole time but had not said a word. "I will always feed you guys. You should not worry about that." They seemed very relieved. I asked them if Luke was thinking the same thing. They confirmed he was. When I walked into the room I saw Luke talking to himself, still very upset. I grabbed him and held him in my arms "Luke, darling, aren't you a silly cat" I said to him. He looked at me in amazement. "Do you really think that I would not feed you because I may perhaps some day meet someone I really like?" He was still amazed and all he could do was nod. "Don't be so ridiculous Luke. I will always feed you guys. I know it is the most important thing in the world for cats." He sighed in relieve and said "but you know Mommy, we can't talk to a new Daddy." I did not really see how that could be a problem so I said "why not?"

"Well, because we just can't."

"Okay then, if you guys can't, then you can't. I respect that."

"You do?"

"Sure, why not. Besides, who is going to believe me when I tell them I talk to my cats anyway."

"Not a whole lot of people, Mommy."

"I don't think so either, Luke" I said as I hugged him. He put his paws around my neck and gave me a quick lick on my cheek. It almost made me cry. Cats show their genuine affection only on rare occasions and this was one of them.

37.
Fashion Statement

Today Jimmy came home with a shaved butt. Yes, a shaved butt. And it's not just shaved; it's shaved in a pattern. It just looks horrible. I asked him what that was for. He told me it was the latest fashion on the street. Maya joined the conversation and saw what Jimmy had done "ooh that is so cool" she exclaimed "can I have that also Mommy?"

"I don't think so, Maya."

"Why not! It is so cool!"

"You really think so?"

"Oh yeah, it is the greatest things in the world."

"Well, you are not getting it."

Of course that was the wrong thing to say. I think that in a way, cats are just like children. I mean if I just think back how I was as a teenager. You always want the things you are not allowed to have. Tattoo's, purple punk hair, worn down jeans, make-up and whatever else you can think up to annoy your parents. Maya is no different from a teenage daughter in that sense. But I was not letting her shave her butt in some weird pattern, no matter how "cool" it was. It is funny though how I don't have a problem with Jimmy doing it even though I think it is horrible. I do have a big problem with Maya doing it. Why is that?

Why are we more protective of our girls than of our boys? Are women indeed the weaker sex? I don't think so and yet I do the same as every other parent. I won't let Maya do the same things as Jimmy. And we are talking about cats here. It's a good thing I don't have a teenage daughter, she would probably be locked up in her bedroom all day. She would only come out to go to school. And then the boys that are coming to date Maya. I have seen them on the wall around my house. Life for cats is totally different than for humans. Cats don't get their hearts broken when the relationship goes bad. They just move on to the next one. We humans on the other hand need weeks, months or sometimes even years to heal the pain of loosing someone we love. That loss can be just the break-up of a relationship or someone passing on to the next life. Cats and dogs just move on.

I remember when Vincent died, Angel cried with me that day, but the next day he was over it. I asked him if that meant that he had forgotten all about Vincent. He said he hadn't but there was nothing he could do about it but just go on with his life. "But don't you miss him?" I noticed that he could not really answer that question. So I asked Ari if he would miss his brother if he would pass away. "Why would I miss him?" "Why not? You guys almost always sleep together. You play together. Wouldn't you miss that?" He thought about it for a while and concluded that even though he would miss him, there would be nothing he could do about it. "Then why would you beat yourself up about it?"

But it's not always true. Animals do miss each other or their owners. I remember when I was a little girl that my neighbors had a big dog. One day they went on vacation for a month and the dog stopped eating the day they left. I saw him get worse and worse as time went on. They had left him in good care of a family member who adored the dog and took really good care of him, but the dog just refused to eat. He died the day before they came back from vacation. I have heard stories about dogs being so close to each other that when one died the other followed soon after. I wonder how that will be with Angel and Nero. They are very close as well.

I think it has to do with an inner connection you have with that other person or animal. Some beings are so connected that they cannot live without each other. Like my neighbors' dog, he was so connected to his owners; he could not live without them. I've seen it happen with humans as well. Sometimes when the love of your life passes away you just don't want to continue to live on. But that is a whole other kind of book, I guess.

I was talking about shaved cat butts. Why do my cats always have to do these weird things? I mean, first I have this Maya who wears my jewelry. Then I have Mozes on drugs. I also have a cat that has his own one cat show. There is one that schemes other cats and animals out of their money. And now I have one that shaves his butt. I once asked myself why I can never have a normal cat or a dog for that matter. Why are all my animals weird? Is it me? Do I attract weird animals, or do they get that way when they are with me? Should I examine myself more closely or should I just assume that it's not me, but them.

I looked at Jimmy as he was showing his butt to all the other cats and I said to him "Why did you do that Jimmy?"

He looked at me and said "It's the latest fashion statement, Mommy!"

"If they say that the latest fashion statement is jumping off a building to your death, would you do that?"

They all looked at me to see if I was kidding.

"Jumping off a building is never a fashion statement, Mommy" Ari said to me.

"It's not?"

"Not really. No!" I don't know who said that.

"Could you explain the difference to me?"

They all looked at each other as if to decide who was going to explain to "stupid" Mommy the difference between a fashion statement and jumping off a building. It was Bear who decided to give it a go.

"Okay, you don't die from shaving your butt" he said thinking that it would end the discussion.

"I don't know about that" I said "with a bare butt like that you could catch pneumonia and die." I looked at all of them and saw that I had shocked the entire cat population.

"Can you die from a shaved butt?" Maya wanted to know.

"Of course you can't" Ari had to say something now as well.

"I don't know about that. It is rather cold with a bare butt like that." They all looked at Goofy who had made that last comment. Obviously they were not very happy with him.

Luke: "I think that Mommy is just kidding us about this."

Bear: "You think so?"

"I sure hope so" Jimmy said with a quivering voice. As I looked at him I saw that my statement had really upset him.

"I sure hope so too" Mozes said "what a horrible way to go."

At that point I broke it off. These cats do have a flair for the dramatic and I did not want to upset Jimmy any more. "You will probably not die from a shaved butt, but I was just trying to make a point."

"And your point would be?" Luke demanded to know.

"Why would you do something just because someone else does it?" They all looked at me as in pure amazement. Had I gone mad? Of course you had to do something that someone else did. How else did you fit in?

"But why are you so desperate to fit in?" I asked. More amazed looks.

"It is of the utmost importance to fit in" Jimmy explained, as far as you call that an explanation.

"What is wrong with a little individuality?"

That made them all sigh. I guess, that fitting in is essential for cats. I was not getting anywhere in this conversation so I ended it by telling Maya that she was not shaving her butt while she was living under my roof. I also said that I did not want any of the others shaving their butts. I told them I thought it looked horrible and I was not going to be embarrassed like that.

I think that got through to them. Being embarrassed is something they can relate to. I seem to embarrass them all the time. At least they accuse me of it all the time. I sure hope I am not going to see any more shaved cat butts and I hope Jimmy's hair grows back really fast.

38.
What a difference a year makes

Today I filed the papers for my divorce; a big milestone in my life. I did not tell the boys about what is going to happen. I don't really think they understand the concept of divorce anyway. Besides, they seem happy with the way things are. In the beginning it was strange for them not having their Daddy around (that is when they found out about it), but that is the beauty with animals. They adapt pretty easily, don't over think situations and accept the way things change.

As I sit here on my front porch I just realized that it is exactly one year ago that Vincent died. It is also one year ago that I was so very depressed. I was lucky in the sense that my depression was a result of my thyroid problems. With the right medication I managed to get over it; that and a completely different and healthy lifestyle.

A year ago I did not think I would ever be able to live a normal life again. And today I filed my divorce papers and I can't really say I am very upset about it. A lot has happened in this last year and all I can say is that things have only gotten better. Perhaps this is strange to hear from someone who is just getting a divorce, but believe me when I say that it is for the better. Whenever someone says to me "I'm so sorry" I tell them not to be. It was fun while it lasted but now it's over.

Things had not been going well between the two of us for a very long time. However with me being sick it was rather difficult to do what we both felt was the right thing, namely to separate. Sometimes you stick together even though you know deep down in your heart that things are not going well. Okay, the dishes did not fly through the house, but there was much stress on a different level. The day he moved out was a great relief for me. Of course it took some getting used to. Being alone all of a sudden when you have never been alone in your entire life is terrifying.

Over the past few months I have done a lot of thinking, which is natural of course. You go through all the emotions one can possibly think of, loneliness, sadness, anger, hopelessness, frustration and any other emotion that is out there. You blame yourself for your failing marriage, you blame him. Because let's face it, most people don't want to fail at anything they do. You try to figure out where you went wrong and you also remember the good times and you say to yourself, "it wasn't all bad". I know where things went wrong and I know what not to do next time I meet someone. I am sure there will be new mistakes to make in my next relationship. That is, if there is a next relationship. Because looking to the future I can honestly say that it is scary. All kinds of questions race through your head. Will I ever find someone to share my life with? Will I remain single for the rest of my life? Will I have the guts to start a new relationship with someone? What will it be like to fall in love again? What will the future bring me in terms of work and career? Where will I be in a year from now? Will I be able to do it all on my own?

Over the past few months I have been thinking a lot about my father as well. He raised me to be a fighter and I think that I have proven that I am. I've overcome the worst and will keep on fighting. Things are definitely not easy when you are trying to get your life back on track. But I am confident about the future and I know that I will manage to do what I set my mind to. My fathers' death had a deep impact on my life and it is only natural that I think a lot about him during these difficult days. I think that if he sees how I am doing, he will be proud of me. I sometimes just wish I could have a chat with him and get some feedback. Alas, this is not possible, so I rely on my friends for the feedback. And what a great bunch they are!

As I was sitting here thinking about the past year, Aristotle came to sit next to me on the table and as always started reading what I was writing. He does that pretty often. Mainly because he is worried I will write bad things about him. But he also does it because he is just plain nosy. He always has to know what is going on, and what is happening. Whenever I go out, I always get an entire questionnaire. As always I ignore him, and he gets angry with me, which I solve with some cat nibbles. If only human relations were solved that easily. But today he looked at me after reading the first page and said "What is divorce?"

"Divorce means that Mommy and Daddy won't be married anymore."

"I see. Does that mean Daddy won't be living here anymore?"

"It means exactly that, dear."

"Does this mean you two hate each other?"

"No, we don't hate each other."

"Well if you don't hate each other you can live together."

"Not really, darling. In order for humans to live together as man and woman they should do more than just "like" each other."

"Well, I like my brother and we live together."

"I know, but you don't really have a choice there do you?"

He had to think about that one for a second after which he said "Yes I do. If I wanted I could live somewhere else."

I just looked at him. I was not about to explain to him that he really did not have a choice, but as I was about to say something more about the situation he said "It's just weird, Mommy. The two of you have been together for as long as I am alive."

"I know that dear, but we just couldn't work it out."

"You are not even going to try for the sake of your children?"

"Not really. We are divorcing and you guys are all staying with me. Can you live with that?"

"Are those dumb dogs staying as well?"

"Yes, they are." He sighed heavily as if he was resigning himself to a terrible fate. Cats can be so dramatic at times.

At that point Luke jumped on the table and asked what was going on. "Mommy is divorcing" Ari informed him. "I see" Luke said "when are we eating dinner?" I smiled, I was glad to see that another one of my cats had his priorities straight. It's weird enough that my cats talk to me, but these human traits that some of them have are sometimes just plain freaky. They did not make a big deal out of my husband moving out and they were obviously not making a big deal out of the divorce. Tomorrow Ari will have accepted it as well. He just thinks more about humans than the other cats do. That's why his name is Aristotle, my little philosopher.

I do wonder what Clubby would have said about it. Knowing him he would probably have said "you gotta do what you gotta do." He would always say that when we made a decision that was beyond his comprehension. It would make me smile. This stoic acceptance of the world around him made life easier for him. Some cats really get upset when things change around them. Clubby always accepted changes for what they were and made the best of them. I always try to do the same; accept changes for what they are and make the best of them. Is there any other way to deal with something like this? My other option would be to wallow in self-pity and look at life as a constant struggle. I don't think that would be the right way. Face life as a challenge, and conquer it!

As I sit here on my front porch thinking about the past year, I can only conclude that one year can make a big difference. Heck, even a few weeks in your life can make a big difference. It makes me wonder where I will be in a year from now. I think it will be an exciting journey!

39.
The final chapter

Goofy is having some trouble with one of the kittens at school. Well to be more specific, with one of the parents of the kittens. Some custody battle is going on for one of the kittens, and now the father (the cat father that is) is trying every day to get his kitten from school. The mother has asked Goofy not to let the kitten go with his father, so that is what he has been trying. However Goofy is not a fighter. He is really sweet and this kitten's father is a real bully.

Two days ago Goofy came home and he was limping. I asked him what happened and he told me that he was beaten up by this father cat. Now he has asked Luke to stand guard. Having worked as the bouncer at Bear's club, this is right up Luke's alley, so he gladly accepted. Any reason to get into a fight is a good reason according to him.

Maya does not like Luke being at Goofy's school at all. For some reason he is always mean to her in situations like that. I think the trouble she caused at the Cat concert is responsible for that. Luke just wants to make sure he doesn't get the same problems. Guess his methods of keeping order are not the most sophisticated ones. But what was more interesting was why Maya would be at a kitten school, so I asked her. She is, after all, almost 2 years. Kitten school goes till 9 months. She told me she was doing her internship there. "But I thought you were going to be a nurse?" I asked her. Turns out she decided to change careers.

Yesterday afternoon she came home crying because Luke bullied her once again. She sat on my lap for almost an hour before I had her calmed down enough. I promised her I would talk to Luke about it. She knows that I always keep my promises and with this one she finally fell asleep on my lap. I just love having her around. We are the only two women in the house amongst all those men and we have to stick together. She is just such a happy cat and very chatty. For some reason I never get tired of her; always playful and never in a bad mood, just sad sometimes when one of the boys is mean to her.

I think I know why they are like that. They want to protect her. After all she is their little sister and brothers are always protective of their little sister. Even now my brother still feels he has to protect me even though he lives 6000 miles away from me.

I just sat there with her sleeping, enjoying her presence. Have you ever noticed how relaxing it is to have a sleeping cat on your lap? It's the best anti-stress medication you can get.

At the end of the day I suddenly heard the dogs barking really vicious at the back of the yard. I walked over to find out that there was a wild cat in my back yard. He was covered by some dried up grass and growling at the dogs. As I was walking up to them, the boys kept running back and forth between me and the cat. "Tell him to leave Mommy!" they yelled at me. When I got to the cat I suddenly heard Maya behind me "Run

Charlie, run!" I heard the wild cat say "Charlie no run" and he continued to growl at the dogs.

"Who is that Maya?"

"That's Charlie, Mommy."

"And who is Charlie, Maya?"

She giggled and I am sure if possible she would have blushed "Charlie is my boyfriend" she said shyly.

Oh my goodness, not another boyfriend. But then again, you can't blame the cats for wanting to be her boyfriend. She is after all, a very pretty cat.

"What is Charlie doing here, Maya?"

"I told him he could sleep here."

I sighed, just what I needed, my cats inviting other cats to the house. If Bear and Luke saw him they would rip him to pieces. It's weird really, they will accept any kitten that I bring into the house, but they hate every grown-up cat that comes into the yard.

"That is not a good idea, Maya, you know that" I told her.

"Yes, I do Mommy, but I am teaching him to speak human."

"Why?"

"Why not?"

"Never mind, Maya" I sighed "I don't think it's a good thing to have him here, dear. Just look at how the dogs are behaving." Well, that was obviously the wrong argument.

She started on how those dragons should mind their own business. It took me about 5 minutes to calm her down again.

"You know what, Charlie can stay, and I will tell the dogs to leave him alone" and I did just that. The boys just stood there dumbfounded. They feel it is their duty to chase any strange cat off our property.

"Let's go boys" I said to them "Charlie is Maya's friend and he can stay. Leave him alone."

"But… but…"

"No buts just leave him alone and come inside" I said and I walked away.

They stood there in disbelief for a few moments but finally followed me; very hesitantly, I might add. I turned around to see if Charlie was still there and I saw Maya standing close to him and then she turned away and followed me.

"Bye Charlie!" she cried and she ran with me toward the house.

"Bye Mommy!"

"Where are you going Maya" I asked as she was walking away.

"I am going to Jennifer" she answered and she ran away.

That was the last time I saw her. Last night she did not come home and I searched for over an hour. I had the worst possible feeling and did not sleep all night. This morning I got out of bed with a knot in my stomach. I knew something was wrong. It was. I found her dead in the neighbor's yard. Those dogs got to her as they got to Mickey. Needless to say I was devastated.

Today is a bad day. I got home from work early and as I sat in my gazebo crying my eyes out, I saw something moving in the grass. It was Charlie.

"Where Maya?" he said, very clumsily. I just sat there looking at him. Would he be able to understand? Mozes was sitting next to me the entire time and seeing how I was struggling with this he walked over to Charlie. He must have said something that was making sense, because I saw Charlie's face get sadder and sadder. That made me even sadder. Obviously he had really loved her. Even the dogs were sad about her death and they did not even attempt to go after Charlie.

My little Maya; she was my joy for almost two years and in those two years she made a tremendous impact on my life. She will be missed. I will miss her talks at night before going to sleep. I will miss her happy spirit. She will be missed as I miss all my darlings.

Another piece of my heart missing.

FINAL NOTE FROM THE AUTHOR

It took me over two years to write this book. Two very long years that were filled with illness, misfortune and heartache. With a lot of hard work I managed to turn my life around. I was lucky in so many ways to be able to do that. After all those years of sickness I am now finally symptom free and feeling good again. Feeling alive again! And what a sensation that is!

The other day I received an e-mail from a friend that said that people come into your life for a reason, a season or a lifetime. The reason are the people who have come to assist you through a difficulty, to provide you with guidance and support, to aid you physically, emotionally or spiritually. They may seem like a godsend and they are. They are there for the reason you need them to be.

Those that come for a season are there because it is your turn to share, grow or learn. The seasons bring you an unbelievable amount of joy.

And then there is the lifetime. These relationships teach you lifetime lessons and things I must build upon in order to have a solid emotional foundation.

When I read it I realized how true it was. But it doesn't only go for people you meet. It goes for the animals in your life as well. In hindsight everything makes sense. In hindsight I can say that I was seriously ill for 4 years without even realizing how sick. And ever since I started to get ill, people and animals started coming into my life.

Steve and Doreen, you were the first and you stood by me all the way and you have encouraged me constantly to finish this book.

Chris, I bless the day I met you. You are always a great support to me. You know I love you dearly!

The angels were watching over me when they sent me Sherry. You are always there when I need someone to talk to. You are a very wise person Sherry.

And there are so many other people to thank, who will probably be very surprised to see they are mentioned here: Martin, Analia, Linda, Michal, Harry, Arpi, Charise and Peter, you have all helped me more then you will ever know and I am eternally grateful for it. I thank you all, my friends, because without you I would not be where I am today.

So what about the animals you may ask? I started writing this book because of Maya. She was such a happy little kitten; so full of life and playful. In fact I started writing when I had her just a few weeks after I had found her alongside the road. When she died I thought I could never finish this book. Obviously I was wrong. And since she was the reason I started writing this book, I only saw it fitting to make the last chapter about her as well.

Little Vincent came into my life just when I hit rock bottom in May of 2005. Taking care of him for those two weeks, was exactly what I needed to get back on my feet again. It all makes so much sense now. Like I said, in hindsight everything becomes clear. If only we had hindsight sooner.

The stories in this book are somewhat based on facts and actual events. Whenever something happened and I wasn't able or capable to write about it, I would make short notes or lock it away in my memory to write it down when I could. As I write the last lines of this book, a brand new life lays before me. I've overcome the worse and grew stronger because of it.

My life begins now...

Sandra Klein
Aruba
July 2006